W.H.G. Kingston

The Voyages and Travels of Count Funnibos and Baron Stilkin

W.H.G. Kingston

The Voyages and Travels of Count Funnibos and Baron Stilkin

ISBN/EAN: 9783337205324

Printed in Europe, USA, Canada, Australia, Japan

Cover: Foto ©Andreas Hilbeck / pixelio.de

More available books at **www.hansebooks.com**

VOYAGES AND TRAVELS

OF

COUNT FUNNIBOS

AND

BARON STILKIN.

BY THE LATE

W. H. G. KINGSTON,

AUTHOR OF "THE SETTLERS," "THE TWO SHIPMATES," "OWEN HARTLEY," ETC., ETC.

PUBLISHED UNDER THE DIRECTION OF THE
COMMITTEE OF GENERAL LITERATURE AND EDUCATION, APPOINTED BY
THE SOCIETY FOR PROMOTING CHRISTIAN KNOWLEDGE.

LONDON:

Society for Promoting Christian Knowledge,

NORTHUMBERLAND AVENUE, CHARING CROSS;

43, QUEEN VICTORIA STREET, AND 48, PICCADILLY.

NEW YORK: POTT, YOUNG & CO.

VOYAGES AND TRAVELS

OF

COUNT FUNNIBOS AND BARON STILKIN.

CHAPTER I.

"WHAT shall we do with ourselves, my dear Stilkin?" exclaimed Count Funnibos, yawning and stretching out his legs and arms, which were of the longest.

"Do! why, travel," answered Baron Stilkin, with a smile on his genial countenance.

"Travel! what for?" asked the Count, yawning again.

"To see the world, to be sure," answered the Baron.

"The world! why, don't we see it by looking out of the window?" asked the Count.

"That's what many people say, and fancy they know the world when they have looked out of their own windows," observed the Baron.

"Ah, yes, perhaps you are right: you always are when I happen to be wrong, and you differ from me—unless you are wrong also," replied the Count. "But where shall we go?"

"Why, round the world if we want to see it;—or as far round as we can get," said the Baron, correcting himself; "and then we shall not have seen it all."

"When shall we start?" asked the Count, brightening up; "next year?"

"Next fiddlesticks! this afternoon, to be sure. Don't put off till to-morrow what can be done to-day, still less till next year. What's to hinder us? We have no ties."

"Yes, there are my neck-ties to come from the laundress," said the Count, who was addicted to taking things literally; "and I must procure some new shoe-ties."

"Never mind, I'll get them for you in good time," said the Baron. "You have plenty of money, so you can pay for both of us, which will simplify accounts."

"Yes, to be sure, I hate complicated accounts," remarked the Count, who thought the Baron the essence of wisdom, and that this was an especially bright idea. "And what luggage shall we require?"

"Let me see: you have two valises—one will do for you and the other for me," said the Baron, putting his fore-finger on his brow in a thoughtful manner. "Ah, yes; besides the ties you will require a shirt-collar or two, a comb to unravel those hyacinthine locks of yours, a pair of spectacles, and a toothpick. It might be as well also to take an umbrella, in case we should be caught out in the rainy season."

"But shouldn't I take my slippers?" asked the Count.

"What a brilliant idea!" exclaimed the Baron. "And that reminds me that you must of course take your seven-league boots."

"But I have only one pair, and if I put them on I shall be unable to help running away from you, and we could no longer be called travelling companions."

"Ah, yes, I foresaw that difficulty from the first," observed the Baron. "But, my dear Funnibos, I never allow difficulties to stand in my way. I've thought of a plan to overcome that one. You shall wear one boot and I'll wear the other, then hand in hand we'll go along across the country almost as fast as you would alone."

"Much faster—for I should to a certainty lose my way, or stick in a quagmire," observed the Count.

"Then all our arrangements are made," said the Baron. "I'll see about any other trifles we may require. Now let us pack up."

"You have forgotten my ties," observed the Count.

"Ah, yes, so I had," observed the Baron, and he hurried off to the laundress for them. He soon returned, and the valises being filled and strapped up, the Baron tucked one under each arm.

"Stop," said the Count, "I must give directions to my housekeeper about the management of my castle and estates during my absence."

"Tell her to bolt the windows and lock all the doors of the castle, so that no one can get in; and as for the estates, they won't run away," said the Baron.

"Thank you for the bright idea; I'll act upon it," answered the Count. "Still, people do lose their estates in some way or other. How is that?"

"Because they do not look properly after them," answered the Baron.

"But mine are secured to my heirs," said the Count.

"Then they cannot run away unless your heirs run also, therefore pray set your mind at rest on that score; and now come along." The Baron as he spoke took up the two portmanteaus, which were patent Lilliputians, warranted to carry any amount of clothing their owners could put into them, and they set off on their travels.

"In what direction shall we go?" asked the Count.

"That must depend upon circumstances," answered the Baron. "Wherever the wind blows us."

"But suppose it should blow one day in one direction and another in the opposite, how shall we ever get to the end of our voyage?" inquired the Count, stopping, and looking his companion in the face.

"That puzzles me, but let us get on board first, and see how things turn out," observed the Baron. "Ships do go round the world somehow or other, and I suppose if they do not find a fair wind in one place they find it another."

"But how are they to get to that other place?" asked the Count, who was in an inquisitive mood.

"That's what we are going to find out," observed the Baron.

"But must we go by sea?" asked the Count. "Could not we keep on the land, and then we shall be independent of the wind?"

"My dear Count, don't you know that we cannot possibly get round the world unless we go by sea?" exclaimed the Baron. "I thought that you had received a better education than to be ignorant of that fact."

"Ah, yes, to be sure, when I have condescended to look at a map, I have observed that there are two great oceans, dividing the continent of America from Europe on one side, and Asia on the other, but I had forgotten it at the moment. However, is it absolutely necessary to go all the way round the world? Could we not on this excursion just see a part of it, and then, if we like our expedition, we can conclude it on another occasion."

"But how are we to see the world unless we go round it?" exclaimed the Baron, with some asperity in his tone. "That is what I thought we set out to do."

"Ah, yes, my dear Baron, but, to tell you the truth, I do not feel quite comfortable at the thoughts of going so far," said the Count, in a hesitating tone. "Could not we just see one country first, then another, and another, and so on? We shall know far more about them than if we ran round the globe as fast as the lightning flashes, or bullet or arrow flies, or a fish swims; or you may choose any other simile you like to denote speed," observed the Count. "In that case we should only see things on our right hand, and on our left, and I do not think we should know much about the countries towards either of the Poles."

"Your remark exhibits a sagacity for which I always gave you credit," observed the Baron, making a bow to his friend. "But I tell you what, if we stop talking here we shall never make any progress on our journey. Let us go down to the quay and ascertain what vessels are about to sail, and we can accordingly take a passage on board one of them."

"We could not well take a passage on board two," observed the Count.

"Ha, ha, ha!" laughed the Baron; "very good, very good; but come along, my dear fellow; stir your stumps, as the English vulgarly express it; let us be moving; *Allons donc*, as a Frenchman would say." And arm in arm the two travellers proceeded to the quay. On reaching it they observed an indi-

vidual of rotund proportions, with a big apron fastened up to his chin, seated on the end of a wall smoking a long clay pipe, and surrounded by chests, bales, casks, and packages of all descriptions. He looked as if he was lord of all he surveyed: indeed there was no other individual in sight except a person coming up some steps from the river and bringing several buckets suspended from a stick over his shoulders, but he was evidently a hewer of wood and a drawer of water, and therefore of no account in the eyes of the burly gentleman.

"Friend," said the Baron, making a bow to the latter individual, "can you inform me where we shall find a vessel about to sail round the world, and when she is likely to proceed on her voyage?"

The latter individual took a sidelong glance at the Baron, and then at the Count, and blew a puff of smoke, but made no answer.

"The poor man is perhaps deaf," suggested the Count. Whereon the Baron in louder tones exclaimed, "Can you tell me, friend"—the burly individual blew another cloud of smoke—"where shall we find a vessel about to sail round the world, and when she commences her voyage?" continued the Baron.

The burly individual opened his eyes as wide as his fat cheeks would allow him, then blew a fresh cloud of smoke, and with the end of his pipe, evidently not wishing to fatigue himself by speaking, pointed along the quay, where the masts of numerous vessels could be seen crowded together.

"Thank you, friend," said the Count, making a bow, for he always piqued himself on his politeness. The Baron felt angry at not having his question answered more promptly, and only gave a formal nod, of which the burly individual took not the slightest notice.

The two travellers continued on, picking their way among the casks, cases, bales, packages and anchors, and guns stuck upright with their muzzles in the ground, and bits of iron chain and spars, and broken boats, and here and there a capstan or a windlass, tall cranes, and all sorts of other articles such as encumber the wharves of a mercantile seaport. As they went along the Baron asked the same question which he had put to the burly individual of several other persons whom he and his friend encountered; some laughed and did not take the trouble of replying, others said that there were vessels of all sorts about to sail to various lands, but whether they were going round the world was not known to them.

"We must make inquiries for ourselves," said the Baron. "Remember that those who want a thing go for it, those who don't want it stay at home; now, as we do want to know where those ships are about to sail to, we must go."

"But, my dear Baron, a dreadful thought has occurred to me. I quite forgot to speak to Johanna Klack, my estimable and trustworthy housekeeper, to give her directions as to her proceedings during my absence. I really think I must go back, or she will not know what to do."

"No, no, my dear Count, I cannot allow you to do so foolish an act. I know Johanna Klack too well for that," said the Baron, with some bitterness in his tone. "She'll not let you go away again; she'll talk you to death with arguments against your going; she'll lock you up in the blue room, or the brown room, or in the dungeon itself, and I shall have to proceed alone. More than half the pleasure of the voyage will be lost without your society; besides which, I have no money to pay for my passage, for you will remember that you undertook to do that.

"Then, I will leave my portmanteau and my umbrella with you as a security," said the Count, trying to get his arm free from that of his friend.

"Ha, ha, ha! that will be no security at all," observed the Baron. "Why, it would be the cause of my destruction. Just see how I should be situated. Johanna Klack will shut you up, and you will disappear from this sublunary world for a time, at all events. It is already known that we set out on our travels. I shall be discovered with your portmanteau as well as my own, and accused, notwithstanding my protestations of innocence, of having done away with you, and before Johanna Klack allows you to reappear I shall to a certainty be hung up by the neck, or have my head chopped off, or be transported beyond seas. Johanna Klack may be a very estimable and charming individual, but I know her too well to trust her. Let her alone; she and your steward being, as you say, thoroughly honest, will manage your affairs to your satisfaction. When we are once away—two or three hundred miles off—you can write and tell her that you are gone on your travels, and give such directions as you may deem necessary. Come along, my dear fellow, come along; I fear even now that she may have discovered our departure and may consider it her duty to follow us."

"If she does, she had better look out for the consequences," said the Baron to himself.

The Count yielded to his friend's arguments, and they continued their course. As they reached the more frequented parts of the quay, where the larger number of vessels were collected, they observed a party of jovial sailors assembled in front of a wine-shop door; some were seated at their ease on benches, either smoking or holding forth to their companions, who were standing by listening. They looked perfectly happy and contented with themselves. One lolling back with his legs stretched out, who was evidently the orator of the party, and thought no small beer of himself, was spinning

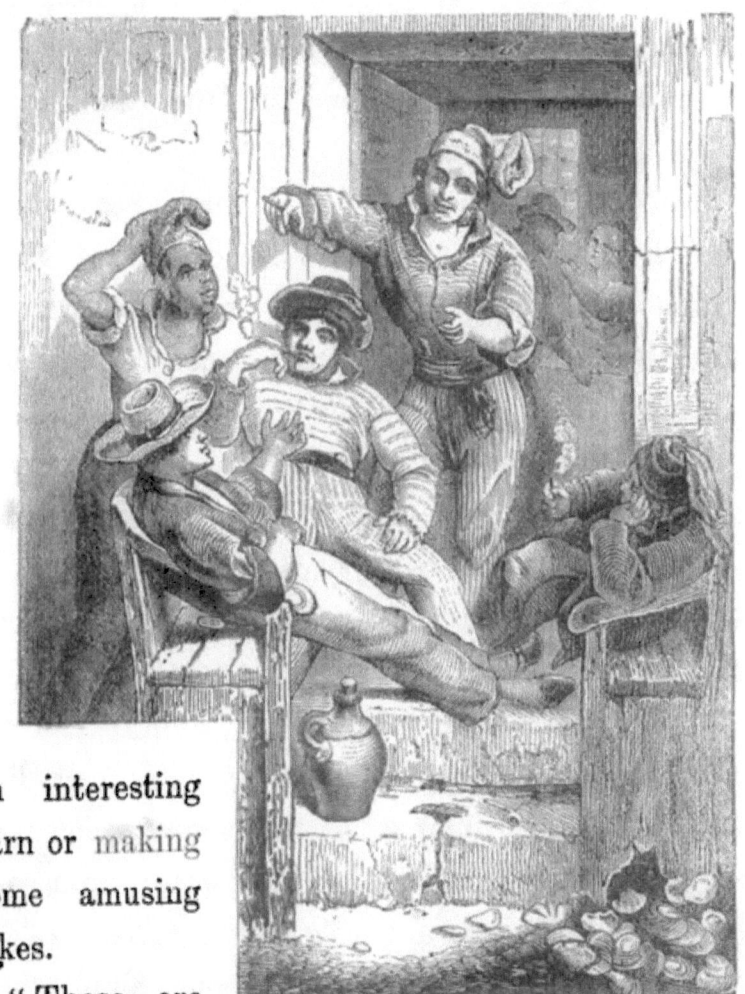

an interesting
yarn or making
some amusing
jokes.

"Those are
the sort of mariners I should like to sail with,"
observed the Baron. "They are stout fellows, and

probably first-rate seamen. Let us draw near and hear what they are talking about."

The sailors took no notice of the Count and Baron as they approached.

"I tell you I've been to the North Sea and to the South Seas, to the Red Sea and the Black Sea, and the Yellow Sea too, and crossed the Atlantic, Pacific, and Indian Oceans scores of times; and I've sailed to the North Pole and South Pole, and all the world round, and I have seen stranger sights than have most men, from the day they were born to the day they died. The strangest spectacle I ever beheld was once in the Indian Ocean. We were sailing along with a fair breeze and studding sails set below and aloft, when we saw coming towards us five water-spouts, just like so many twisted columns: dark clouds seemed to come from the sky, and piles of water rose out of the ocean. It was a bad look-out for us, for we expected to have them aboard our ship, when they would have sent her to the bottom in no time. But our skipper was not a man to be daunted by difficulties. As soon as he saw them coming he ordered the guns to be loaded and run out. As the first came near he fired, and down fell the waterspout with a rushing sound into the ocean. "It is your turn next," he sang out, pointing a gun at another, which he treated in the same fashion ; but three came on together, when he blazed away at them and

all were knocked to pieces in a moment; and the ocean was as calm as it had been before we saw them. You may well say that was curious. I have heard of waterspouts doing much damage, but I never saw a ship swamped by one."

The Count and Baron were much interested, and

got still nearer, that they might not lose a word.

"I told you, mates, that I had been to the North Pole and South Pole, and I've seen wonderful sights there also. What do you think of an iceberg a mile long, two or three hundred feet high? I have been among such, and surrounded by them too, in a way which seemed as if it was impossible we should ever get free again. When the sun is shining they're beautiful to look at: some with great caverns below, with icicles hanging down from the roof, and the top of the berg covered with what one might fancy to be towers, steeples, and ruined castles and arches, all glittering and shining just as if they were made of alabaster and precious stones; and the sea a deep purple, or sometimes blue, with streaks of yellow and red. You'd think it was cold enough there, but the summer up in the North is one long day, with the sun in the sky all the time; and I have known it pretty hot there—hot enough to set the icebergs melting, and the water rushing down their sides in fountains. Now and then, when

the under part is worn away, they get top-heavy,
and over they go, just like a porpoise making a
somersault. It does not do to be near them on
those occasions, for they'd send the stoutest ship
to the bottom in a moment; and even at a distance I have known bits of ice come down on the
deck big enough to crack a blackamoor's head,
though we were many fathoms off it.

" As I said, the summer is short, and that is the
only time ships can sail about, and make their way
among the ice. Then comes the winter, and terribly
long that is; it lasts well nigh ten months, and for
all that time the ship is shut up just as fast as
if she was in a dock with the entrance closed
by stone. There she lies, housed over, with top-
gallant-masts struck, and if it was not for the stoves
below, which must be kept alight at all hours of
the day and night, people would be frozen to death:
I have heard, indeed, of a whole ship's company
being turned into ice. For many days during the
time the sun is below the horizon, and there is
one long night; the stars, however, when the sky

is clear, shine brightly, and sometimes the Northern lights blaze up and sparkle, and people can see

their way over the ice, but it is not pleasant travelling, and one has to wear wonderfully thick clothing, and mits on the hands, and to cover up all but the eyes, nose, and mouth, or a man would get frost-bitten very quickly. Then bears come prowling about, and they are awkward customers to meet alone, for they have powerful jaws and sharp claws, and one hug is

enough to squeeze the breath out of a person.
They have carried off many a poor fellow who
has wandered away from his ship. Besides the
bears there are Arctic foxes, with white fur, and
though they do not attack a fellow on his feet with
a thick stick in his hand, yet I do not know how
they would treat him if they found him lying down
unable to defend himself.

"Sometimes ships, before they can get into
harbour, are caught in the ice, and have to pass
the winter out in the sea, if they have time to
cut a dock before the ice presses on them. They
may thus be tolerably secure, but I have known
ships to be crushed to atoms before they have
had time to do that, and their crews have had
to get on board other ships, or make for the
land, and spend the winter there in snow huts; or
they have perished. Still, many people have passed
two and three winters together in the Arctic
regions, and have kept their health and been
happy, when they have had sufficient firing and
good food. On one of those occasions I learned

to read and write, which I did not know how to
do before, and much use it has been to me ever
since.

"Then we had amusements of all sorts. We
rigged a theatre on board, and acted plays and
recited, and had a masquerade, and funny sort of
dresses we appeared in. But we had work to
do also; we had to build a wall of snow round
the ship, so that in cold weather we were pro-
tected from the wind when we took our exercise,
running round and round inside it. The worst
part of the business was the long night and the
bitter cold, for it was cold, I can tell you; and
glad enough we were when we saw the sun rising
just above the hillocks of ice far away to the
southward, and though for some time it was for
a very short period above the horizon, yet day
after day at noon it appeared higher and higher,
and its rays shed some warmth down upon us.

"Still the winter was not over, and our captain
arranged to make some journeys to explore the
country. In that part of the world dogs are often

used to draw sleighs, but as we had no dogs we
were compelled to drag them ourselves, about five
men to each sleigh, which is a sort of long carriage without wheels, with iron runners like two
skates placed under it, and the goods lashed along
on the top. We carried our provisions, tents, and
cooking uten-
sils. When
the ice was
smooth it was
pretty easy
travelling, but
we often had
to drag the
sleighs up
steep places,
over hillocks,

and rough ground, and then it was heavy work, and
we could only make good a few miles a day.

"A man need be pretty strong and hardy to go
through that sort of work. At night we slept
inside our tents, as close together as we could

pack, the only warmth we could obtain being from the spirit lamps we carried, which served also to warm up our cocoa and cook our food. I was not sorry when the journey was over, though we were merry enough during it. At length we got out of harbour, but we had still not a few dangers to encounter. Sometimes we were nearly driven on shore by the floes of ice pressing on us; at others we ran a great risk of being nipped by getting between two floes which approached each other; then there was the chance of the icebergs falling down on us. We several times had to cut our way with saws through the ice to get into open water. We were heartily glad when we were free altogether, and sailing along with a fair wind over the ocean to the southward, leaving the world of ice astern. However, I should be ready to go again, and so would most fellows who were with me, I have a notion."

"That's more than I should, after what I have heard," observed the Count to the Baron. "I object excessively to take a trip to the North Pole, where-

ever else we may go. I have no fancy, either, to be
sent to the bottom by a waterspout."

"Wherever we go we may expect to meet with
some danger or other," said the Baron. "It adds
zest to the pleasure of travelling."

"I would rather avoid the zest," said the Count. "But shall we ask these brave fellows what ship they belong to. Perhaps she's not going to the North Pole or the Indian Seas on this occasion, and they evidently form a sturdy crew. Will you speak to them or shall I?"

"I'll address them," said the Baron, and stepping up to the seamen, he said—

"Brave sailors, I have heard the account your shipmate has been giving you of his adventures, and as we are desirous of sailing round the world, we should be glad to take a passage on board the ship to which you belong."

"Unless you were to chop yourselves up into a good many portions you'd find that a hard matter, master," answered one of the seamen. "We all happen, do ye see, to belong to different ships, and some don't belong to any ship at all, and when we do sail, the chances are we go to as many parts of the world."

"Then, most gallant sailors, will you have the kindness to inform us what ship is likely next to sail from this port, and whither is she bound?" said the Baron.

"As to that, I heard old Jan Dunck, skipper of the galiot *Golden Hog*, saying that he was about to sail for Amsterdam with the next tide. It wants but an hour or so to that time, and if you look sharp about it you may get on board and make your arrangements with him before he trips his anchor," answered the sailor.

"Thanks, brave sailors, for the information you have afforded us," said the Baron. "You will confer a further favour if you will show us where the said galiot *Golden Hog* lies at anchor. Among this vast fleet of shipping we should otherwise have considerable difficulty in discovering her, and my friend Count Funnibos will, I am sure, reward you handsomely."

"Reward is neither here nor there, but I don't mind showing you old Dunck's craft, if you will come along with me."

Thus saying, the sailor, getting up, put his hands in his pockets, and led the way along the quay. On one side it was bordered by high houses, with curious gables; the floors projecting one beyond the other, and little terraces and balconies and excrescences of all sorts, carved and painted in gay colours, and cranes and beams, with blocks and ropes hanging from their ends. On the other side appeared a forest of masts, yards, and rigging, rising out of vessels of all shapes and sizes, in apparently such inextricable confusion that it seemed impossible they should ever get free of each other, and float independently on the ocean. On the opposite side was an old castle with four towers, looking very glum and gloomy; and more vessels and boats below it, leaving the centre of the river tolerably clear for other craft to pass up and down. The sailor rolled along with an independent air, not looking to see whether those he had offered to guide were following him; now and then, when passing an old shipmate it might be, or other nautical acquaintance, he gave a nod of recognition without taking his hands from his pockets or his pipe from his mouth.

" Who have you got
in tow there?" asked
one or two.

" Don't know: they
want to see the skipper,
Jan Dunck, and I'm
piloting them to where his galiot lies."

" They look remarkably green, but they'll be

done considerably brown before old Dunck lands
them," he said in an under tone, so that the Count
and Baron did not hear him. As they were going
along the sailor stopped suddenly, and pointed to a
black-whiskered man, wearing a tarpaulin hat on
his head, with high boots, and a flushing coat.

" There's the skipper, Jan Dunck, and there's his
craft just off the shore. I'll tell him what you want,
and wish you a good voyage," said the seaman, who
then went up to the skipper.

" If they pay for their passage, and do not
complain of the roughness of the sea, or blame me
for it, I'll take them," said the skipper, eyeing the
Count and the Baron as he spoke.

The arrangement was soon concluded.

" But you promised that I should reward the
sailor," observed the Count to his friend.

" I will return him our profuse thanks. Such
will be the most simple and economical way of
paying the debt," answered the Baron; and turning
to the seaman, he said, politely lifting his hat,
" Most brave and gallant mariner, Count Funnibos

and Baron Stilkin desire to return you their most profuse thanks for the service you have rendered them, in conducting them this far on their journey, and making known to them this, I doubt not, worthy, stout, and sturdy captain, with whom they are about to commence their voyages over the treacherous ocean."

"That's neither here nor there; I was happy to do you a service and you're welcome to it, only in future don't make promises which you cannot pay in better coin than that you have treated me with; and so good day, Count Fuddlepate and Baron Stickum, or whatever you call yourselves," answered the sailor; who, sticking his pipe in his mouth, which he had taken out to make this long speech, and putting his hands in his pocket, rolled back to where he had left his companions, to whom he failed not to recount the liberal treatment he had received in the way of compliment from the two exalted individuals he had introduced to Captain Jan Dunck.

CHAPTER II.

WELL, Mynheers, the sooner we get on board the galiot the better," said Captain Jan Dunck, addressing the Count and Baron. " She's a fine craft—a finer never floated on the Zuyder Zee; she carries a wonderful amount of cargo ; her accommodation for passengers is excellent; her cabin is quite a palace, a fit habitation for a king.   She's well found with a magnificent crew of sturdy fellows, and as to her captain, I flatter myself—though it is I who say it —that you will not find his equal afloat; yes, Mynheers, I say so without vanity. I've sailed, man and boy, for forty years or more on the stormy ocean, and never yet found my equal.   I will convey you and your luggage and all other belongings to Amsterdam with speed and safety, always providing the winds are favourable, and we do not happen to stick on a mud-bank to be left high and dry till the next spring-tide, or that a storm does not arise and send us to the bottom, the fate which has overtaken many a stout craft, but which by my skill and knowledge I hope to avoid. However, I now invite you to come on board the *Golden Hog*, that we may be ready to weigh anchor directly the tide turns, and proceed on our voyage. There lies the craft on board which you are to have the happiness of sailing;" and Captain Jan Dunck, as he spoke, pointed to a galiot of no over large proportions which lay a short distance from the wharf, with her sails loosed ready for sea.

"Well, we are fortunate in finding so experienced a navigator," observed the Count to the Baron, as they followed Captain Jan Dunck towards the steps at the bottom of which lay his boat. "He'll carry us as safely round the world as would have done the brave Captains Schooten and Le Maire, or Christofero Columbo himself."

"If we take him at his own estimation he is

undoubtedly a first-rate navigator; but you must
remember, my dear Count, that it is not always
safe to judge of men by the report they give of
themselves; we shall know more about them at the
termination of our voyage than we do at present,"
observed the Baron. "However, there is the boat,
and he is making signs to us to follow him."

The Count and Baron accordingly descended the
steps into the galiot's boat, in the stern of which
sat the Captain, his weight lifting the bows up
considerably out of the water. A sailor in a woollen
shirt who had lost one eye, and squinted with
the other, and a nose, the ruddy tip of which
seemed anxious to be well acquainted with his
chin, sat in the bows with a pair of sculls in his
hand ready to shove off at his captain's command.

"Give way," said the skipper, and the one-eyed
seaman began to paddle slowly and deliberately, for
the boat was heavily weighted with the skipper
and the Count and Baron in the stern, and as
there was no necessity for haste, greater speed
would have been superfluous.

"Is this the way boats always move over the water?" asked the Count, as he observed the curious manner in which the bow cocked up.

"Not unless they have great men in the stern, as my boat has at present," answered the skipper.

"Ah, yes, I understand," said the Count, looking very wise.

The boat was soon alongside the galiot, on board which the skipper stepped. As soon as he was out of her the bow of the boat came down with a flop in the water. He then stood ready to receive the Count and Baron. As he helped them up on deck, he congratulated them on having thus successfully performed the first part of their voyage. "And now, Mynheers," he continued, "I must beg you to admire the masts and rigging, the yellow tint of the sails, the bright polish you can see around you."

"You must have expended a large amount of paint and varnish in thus adorning your vessel," observed the Count.

"I have done my best to make her worthy of her

Captain," answered the skipper, in a complacent tone, "and worthy, I may add, of conveying such distinguished passengers as yourselves."

The Count bowed, and the Baron bowed, as they prepared to follow the skipper down through a small square hole in the deck with a hatch over it.

"Why, this is not as grand as I had expected," observed the Count. "Not quite a palace, as you described it, Captain."

"But it is as comfortable as a palace, and I find it far more so in a heavy sea," observed the skipper. "For you must understand that if the vessel gives a sudden lurch, it is a great blessing not to be sent fifty feet away to leeward, which you would be if you were in the room of a palace. See what comfort we have got here—everything within reach. A man has only to rise from his chair and tumble into bed, or tumble out of bed, and sit down in his chair to breakfast. Then, when he dresses he has only to stretch out his hand to take hold of the things hanging up against the bulkhead."

While the skipper was pointing out to his passengers the super-excellence of the accommodation his vessel afforded, a female voice was heard exclaiming, in shrill tones—

"I must see him, I must see my master, the Count! He has bolted, decamped, run off without so much as saying why he was going, or where he was going, or leaving me those full and ample directions which I had a right to expect."

"Hark!" exclaimed the Count, turning pale. "That must be Johanna Klack; if she once sees me, she'll take me back, to a certainty. Oh dear me, what shall I do?"

"I know what I will do," cried the Baron, beginning to ascend the companion-ladder. "Captain Jan Dunck, keep the Count down here below; don't let him show himself on any account. I will settle the matter. This female, this termagant, will carry off one of your passengers, and, as an honest man, you are bound to protect him."

"Ja, ja," said the Captain; "slip into one of those bunks and you will be perfectly safe, and if she manages to get down below, my name isn't Jan Dunck." Saying this, the skipper followed the Baron up on deck, and, clapping on the hatch, securely bolted it.

The Baron had grasped a boathook, the skipper seized a broomstick, and in a loud voice shouted to his crew, "Boarders! repel boarders!" In a boat alongside stood a female, her countenance flushed and irate, showing by her actions her intention of climbing up the vessel's side. The crew obeyed their commander's call, and from the fore hatchway appeared the small ship's boy, holding a kettle of boiling water in his hand, while the rest had armed themselves with various weapons.

"Who are you, and what do you want?" asked Captain Jan Dunck, in a loud voice.

"I am that most ill-used person, Johanna Klack, the housekeeper, once honoured, respected, and trusted, of the noble Count Funnibos, who has been inveigled away with treachery and guile by that false friend of his, the Baron Stilkin. I've proof positive of the fact, for as I hurried along searching for the truant

I met a brave mariner, who told me that he had not only spoken with them, but had seen them go on board this very vessel, and that, if I did not make haste, I should be too late to catch them. There's the Baron; I know him well, and I am very sure that my master is not far off. I must have him, I will have him back!" and, making a spring, she endeavoured to mount the side of the vessel.

"Will you?" exclaimed the skipper, bestowing a rap on her knuckles which made the poor woman let go her hold of the rigging.

"Give it her," cried the Baron, lunging at her with his boathook, at which the small ship's boy rushed forward with the steaming kettle in his hand.

The unfortunate Johanna Klack, alarmed at what might be the consequences, sprang back to the other side of the boat, and, losing her balance, overboard she went, amid the jeers of the hard-hearted skipper and crew of the galiot *Golden Hog*. The hapless Vrouw, as she descended into the far from limpid water, screamed loudly for help, the waterman who had brought her off being too much astonished at first to render it.

"Shove off," cried the skipper, "and hook the woman out of the water, but do not bring her alongside this vessel again, if you value your skull."

The man obeyed, and, stretching out his boathook, got hold of the Vrouw's garments and hauled her on board. The moment she had recovered her breath she insisted on being taken back to the galiot; but the old boatman was suddenly seized with a fit of deafness, and wisely pulled away in an opposite direction.

"Take me back! take me back!" cried Johanna Klack.

"I am rowing as hard as I can," answered the boatman.

"Take me back to the vessel, on board which my honoured master is a prisoner," shouted Johanna Klack.

"We shall soon be at the shore; you can then run home and change your wet garments," answered the old boatman.

"I tell you I want to go back to that vessel," cried the housekeeper, getting more and more angry and excited.

"Ja, ja, Vrouw; ja, ja, I will land you presently."

All this time the boatman was observing the threatening gestures of Captain Jan Dunck and Baron Stilkin. At last he disappeared with his fare behind a crowd of vessels.

"Now, Captain," said the Baron, "the sooner we put to sea the better, for I know Johanna Klack well enough to be certain that, if she does not come herself, she will send a *posse comitatus*, or a party of constables, or some other myrmidons of the law to arrest us under some false accusation or other, and we shall be carried on shore ignominiously as prisoners, and your voyage will be delayed."

"Ja, ja, I understand all about that," answered Captain Jan Dunck. "You boy, with the kettle of boiling water, go and carry it below, and help to get the galiot under weigh. Mate, turn the hands up and make sail."

The crew consisted of the mate, the one-eyed

mariner, and the small ship's boy. The mate and the one-eyed mariner were on deck; they had only to turn up the small ship's boy, who quickly made his appearance on being summoned, and they set to work to turn round the windlass, which soon won the anchor from its oozy bed. The sails were set, and as a light breeze had just then sprung up, the galiot began to move slowly down the canal towards the open ocean, which was yet, however, a good way off. As the breeze freshened the galiot moved faster and faster, and soon the town, with its church steeples and old towers and its crowd of shipping, was left behind.

"I think we might venture to let the Count up on deck," observed the Baron. "He must be pretty well stifled by this time down in the hot cabin."

"Ja, ja," answered Captain Dunck; "let him up. No fear of the Vrouw Klack coming after him now; if she does, we shall see her at a distance, and make preparations for her reception."

"But if she comes with a *posse comitatus*," asked the Baron; "what shall we do then?"

"Send the *posse comitatus* about their business," answered Captain Dunck, flourishing a handspike. "I am skipper of this vessel, and no one shall step on board without my leave, or if they do I will trundle them overboard without their leave.   Oh, oh, oh; let them just come and try it."

On receiving this assurance from Captain Jan Dunck, the Baron, withdrawing the hatch, called to the Count to come on deck, and enjoy the fresh air and the beauty of the scenery.   As no answer was returned, the Baron, beginning to feel alarmed, fearing that his friend had been truly suffocated, descended into the cabin.   A loud snore assured him that the Count was fast asleep, forgetful of his castle, forgetful of the Vrouw Klack, forgetful where he was, and of all other sublunary matters.

"Count Funnibos, come and see the beautiful scenery," shouted the Baron.   Whereon, the Count starting up, hit his head such a blow against the woodwork close above, that he fell back almost stunned.   He, however, soon recovered, and in a low voice asked the Baron what had happened.

"The last thing that has happened is that you gave your head a tremendous thwack," said the Baron; "but my object is to invite you on deck to enjoy the beautiful scenery we are passing through, before we put out into the open ocean, when we shall see no more green fields."

Thus summoned, the Count, getting out of the bunk, accompanied the Baron on deck. Then taking out his note-book he wrote: "Green fields, green trees, windmills pretty numerous, cows white and black still more so, sky and sea as usual, with here and there a vessel or other craft on the calm surface of the latter."

"I see nothing more to describe," he said, as he closed the book and returned it to his pocket.

Still the galiot glided on.

"It strikes me that there is some monotony in this kind of scenery," observed the Count to the Baron; "but it's pleasing, charming, and soothing to one's troubled soul."

At last the wind dropped, and the galiot lay becalmed.

"What are we going to do now?" asked the Count, finding that the vessel no longer moved through the water.

"Drop our anchor and wait till the ebb makes again, unless we wish to be driven up by the flood all the way we have come," observed the skipper.

"What, and run the risk of meeting Johanna Klack!" exclaimed the Count, in a voice of alarm. "By all means do come to an anchor, my dear Captain."

"That's what I intend to do," he answered; and he ordered the anchor to be let go.

Other vessels were in the same condition as themselves, so they had no reason to complain. The scenery was not particularly enlivening, though there were a few trees on the shore; but they were generally stunted in their growth, and bent by the winds. Here and there a small boat appeared, the occupants being engaged either in fishing, or in rowing across the river. One or two people were enjoying the luxury of bathing, and a man

came down to fill a jar
with salt water, probably
to bathe the limbs of one
of his children.

"How long are we
likely to remain here,
Captain Jan Dunck?" in-
quired the Count.

"As I said before, and say it again, till the

tide turns or the breeze springs up," answered the skipper. "What a hurry you appear to be in. The mariners in these seas have to learn patience —a valuable quality under all circumstances. If we grumbled every time we had a calm, or a foul wind, or stuck on a mudbank, we should never cease grumbling."

"Suppose, Captain, as we have nothing else to do, you or one of your crew would be good enough to spin us a yarn," said the Count.

"One-eyed Pieter will spin you a yarn which will last into the middle of next week," said the skipper.

"Then I think that he had better not begin," observed the Count; "for I hope before that time we shall be indulging in fresh milk and eggs on shore."

"You do, do you, noble sir?" said the one-eyed mariner, winking at the mate, or rather intending to do so, for he winked in an opposite direction, as was his custom, though he was unconscious of it. "We're not out of the Scheldt yet, and if we don't get a fair wind, it will be a pretty long time before we reach the Texel and get into the Zuyder Zee."

"Ja, ja; one-eyed Pieter speaks but the truth. You must be prepared, when navigating the changeful ocean, to meet with foul winds as well as fair ones," said the Captain. "Remember that I undertook only to convey you to your destination wind and weather permitting. No skipper ever takes passengers on any other terms."

"I am prepared for whatever Fate wills," said the Count, folding his hands.

"And so am I," said the Baron. "And now I propose, as it is getting late, and I feel sleepiness stealing over my eyelids, that we turn into our bunks and resign ourselves to the keeping of the drowsy god."

"I don't know what you mean by talking of the drowsy god," said the skipper. "As far as I can make out, you intend to take a snooze; that's the best thing you can do."

The Count and the Baron accordingly turned into

their berths (not knocking their heads more than half-a-dozen times as they did so), and were very soon snoring away in concert. So ended the first day of their voyages and travels.

CHAPTER III.

"A FAIR wind, Mynheers! a fair wind!" shouted Captain Jan Dunck down the cabin skylight. "Rouse up, rouse up; come on deck and see how the *Golden Hog* is walking along."

"Walking along, what does he mean? do ships walk?" asked the Count, as, having turned out of his bunk and rubbed his eyes and yawned and stretched himself, he was beginning to dress.

"I suppose it is a nautical expression describing the rapid way a ship moves through the water," observed the Baron. "But we will inquire of the worthy skipper when we get on deck."

"Yes, and I will enter the expression in my notebook," observed the Count.

The travellers were soon on deck. The galiot was gliding rapidly though smoothly through the somewhat yellow waters of the Scheldt. Land could be seen on both sides, but at a considerable distance, for it was here very broad, with villages, towers, curiously-formed landmarks, and here and there a few trees scattered about, just rising above the surface.

"We shall soon come off Vlissingen on our right, which the English call Flushing. It is the last place where, should you be tired of voyaging, I can land you," said the skipper. "You must make up your mind therefore at once, as I shall not touch at another till we come off Brill, at the mouth of the Maas."

"No, no; the Count and I are determined to continue our voyage," answered the Baron; who, having discovered that Captain Jan Dunck had a store of good things on board, had no intention of leaving the vessel, and therefore did his best to dissuade his friend from setting foot on shore even

when the galiot dropped her an- chor off one of the quays of Flushing. Not far off was a landing-place, and people were hurrying up and down, and some even came off and endeavoured to persuade the travellers to come on shore and take up their abode at one of the hotels, where they were assured every comfort and luxury could be obtained at the most moderate prices. The Baron, however, declined for himself and his friend, being somewhat suspicious that, should they leave the galiot, Captain Jan Dunck might become oblivious of their existence and sail without them. In a short time the skipper himself returned, bringing off a quarter of mutton, a round of beef, several baskets of vegetables, half-a-dozen round, cannon-ball-like cheeses of ruddy complexion, bread, and other articles capable of supplying the wants of the inner man. The Baron's eyes glistened, and the Count gazed with satisfaction at the supply of food handed up on deck.

"Why, Captain, you seemed anxious just now to induce us to quit your vessel, and now you bring this magnificent supply of good things," said the Baron, patting his back.

"I was anxious to be rid of you," answered the skipper, frankly. "Judging by the appetite you exhibited at breakfast this morning, you would have very soon eaten up all the provisions intended for the voyage; and one of two things I had to do—either to get rid of you and your companion, or to obtain sufficient food for your nourishment. I tried the first without success—go you would not, and I have now therefore been compelled to adopt the other alternative; hence this stock of provisions. Ja, ja, you understand. But here comes the breeze, we must not lose it. Up anchor, Pieter!"

Pieter, the mate, and small ship's boy, went to the windlass, while the skipper stood at the helm. The galiot was soon got under weigh, and off she glided, not very fast at first, with her head towards the North Sea.

In a short time Flushing, with the masts and yards of its shipping, was lost to sight, and the galiot began ploughing the waters of the North Sea. Fortunately, the wind being off the land, it was tolerably smooth, and she glided on without inconveniencing her passengers.

"What is out there?" asked the Count, pointing across the apparently boundless waters towards the west.

"Thereabouts lies that little island I spoke of inhabited by the English people," answered the skipper. "I hope they may keep to their island, and not come bothering us as they used to do in days of yore. All we want now is to be let alone, aud to be allowed to carry on our commercial affairs like peaceable and well-disposed people—to build our dykes and to cultivate the soil. Think what we have done! We have won half of our country from the sea, and have converted the other half, once no better than a marsh, into dry land. Look at our magnificent towns, our canals, our green fields, our gardens and orchards, and just think what our industry has accomplished. A Dutchman has a right to be proud of his country, and so we are, and intend to defend it, as we always have done, to the last drop of our blood."

The skipper, who grew enthusiastic, was standing at the helm, and he puffed away at his pipe till from the clouds of smoke that ascended the galiot might have been taken at a distance for a steamer.

"Holland is but a small country, though," observed the Count.

"Yes, granted; but it has a large soul. Every inch of its soil is cultivated, or made to produce something. Think of the countless herds of cattle it feeds, and the mountains of cheeses shipped every year to all parts of the world, its ingenious toys, its gorgeous tulips, and the oceans of schiedam it supplies to thirsty souls, not to speak of its many other manufactures, which you will have the opportunity of inspecting during your travels. Other people inhabit fertile countries which they found ready prepared for them, we Hollanders have formed ours; we have won it after a fierce battle of long years from the greedy ocean, which is always endeavouring to regain the ground it has lost, but we keep the ocean in check with our wonderful dykes, and make it subservient to our requirements. You showed your wisdom, Mynheers, in determining to visit it before proceeeding to other parts of the world. In my opinion, you'll not wish to go further; it contains amply sufficient to satisfy the desire of your hearts. Ja, ja."

Captain Jan Dunck emitted a vast column of
smoke, and was silent for some minutes. He then
had to take a pull at the main sheet, for the wind
was heading the galiot; he took another and another,
and his countenance wore a less satisfactory aspect
than it had done lately. The galiot began to pitch,
for the seas were getting up, while she heeled over
as much as galiots ever do, they being sturdy craft,
loving upright ways and sailing best before the wind.
If the skipper looked dissatisfied, his passengers were
evidently much more so; their visages grew longer
and longer, their eyes assumed a fleshy hue, their
lips curled, and it needed no experienced physiognomist
to pronounce them unhappy; conversation ceased, they
spoke only in ejaculations such as " Oh! oh! oh!
Oh dear! oh dear! oh dear!"

At last the Baron managed to say, "Ca—a—a—p-
tain, i—i—i—i—sn't there a harbour into which we
can put till this storm is over?"

" Storm, do you call it," laughed the skipper.
"It is only a head wind, and we shall have to
stand out to the eastward into the North Sea

for a few leagues or so, till we can fetch the Texel."

"Oh dear! oh dear! into the North Sea, did you say?" cried the Count. "How dreadful!"

"Horrible!" exclaimed the Baron.

"Detestable!" cried the Count.

"Well, Mynheers, to please you, remember, seeing that the galiot is likely to make as much leeway as she does headway, we will put into Brill, a town just now on our starboard hand, a short distance up the Maas. Hands about ship!"

The mate, the one-eyed mariner, and the small ship's boy started up at their Captain's call. The helm was put down, the jib-sheet let fly, and the galiot, after exhibiting some doubt as to whether she would do as was wished, came slowly round, her head pointing to the eastward.

"Why, what has become of the wind?" asked the Count, his visage brightening.

"The sea is much more quiet than it was, because we have just got under the land. See that bank away to windward, that keeps it off us. We shall soon be running up the Maas."

In a few minutes the water became perfectly smooth, the Count and Baron recovered their spirits, and in a short time they arrived off a seaport town on the right bank of the Maas.

"There's nothing very grand to boast of," observed the Count, as he surveyed it through his binoculars.

"It has a history, notwithstanding," observed the skipper. "It was here the first successful blow was struck for liberty, by those daring fellows 'The Beggars of the Sea,' under their gallant leader De la Marck. It is a town of pilots and fishermen, and as brave sailors as ever explored the ocean. Here, also, were born our gallant admirals Van Tromp and De Witt, and its harbour is as fine a one as any along the coast. Say what you like, Mynheers, Brill has as good a right to be proud of itself as many a place with greater pretensions. Do you feel disposed to go on shore and survey its advantages?"

"Thank you," said the Baron, "taking all things into consideration, we will remain where we are; dinner will soon be ready, I think; our appetites are wonderfully sharpened by the sea air, and, remembering the store of provender you brought on board, it would be a bad compliment to you not to stay and help you consume it."

"Ja, ja," said the skipper, "do as you please, I am happy to have your company."

The Baron, at all events, did ample justice to the skipper's dinner, and all three spent the remainder of the day on deck, puffing away with their long pipes in their mouths, till it was difficult to say whether they or the galley fire forward sent forth the thickest wreaths. Notwithstanding this, the Baron declared that he was perfectly ready for supper at the usual hour, after which the two passengers turned into their berths and went to sleep. They were awakened by finding the vessel once more pitching and tumbling about, and, thinking that something was about to happen, they crawled up on deck.

" What's the matter, Captain," exclaimed the Count, in an agitated voice; " is there any danger ? "

" No, but there's no small amount of fear among some of us," answered the skipper in a gruff voice.

"We have got a fair wind, and are once more at sea."

"What is that bright spot up there," asked the Count, pointing to a light which streamed forth on the right hand. "That, why that's the Maas Lighthouse," answered the skipper. "It marks the entrance to the river, and we shall soon round it, and be in the open sea. You'll then have the satisfaction of once more bounding over the heaving wave."

"From previous experience I must own that I would rather escape that satisfaction," observed the Count, making a long face. "Couldn't we manage to make our way through some of the numerous canals which I have heard intersect Holland in all directions?"

"We should have been a week or two, or even a month about it, if we had made the attempt," answered the skipper. "We cannot tack in the canals as we can in the open sea. Now we can stretch away from the land as far as we like and then go about again, till we can head up again for the Helder."

"Oh dear, oh dear, I suppose we must submit to our fate," groaned the Count. "Baron, you have much to answer for, dragging me away from

E

my castle and home comforts and the watchful care of that estimable person Johanna Klack."

"Why, you were in a great hurry to escape from her not long ago," answered the Baron, "and now you find fault with me because the sea happens to be a little rough."

"When I wanted to escape from Johanna Klack we were in smooth water, and I would rather endure the clatter of her tongue than the roaring waves and the howling of the winds."

"It is too late to complain now, Count; regrets are vain things at the best," said the Baron. "Let us be content with the present; see, we're getting close to the lighthouse."

"So we are, I can distinguish it clearly," said the Count. "And, hilloa, look up there at those gnats or moths, or what are they, fluttering about the light?"

"Ha, ha, ha! moths or gnats," laughed the skipper; "why those are birds, sea birds and land birds of all descriptions, who come there for the charitable purpose of being turned into pies and puddings and stews by the light-keepers. All the keepers have to do is to go out and catch them by their legs as they alight on the rails and wring their necks. Our friends up there need have no fear of starving; when the wind blows from the land they get land birds, and when from the ocean sea birds, and as they are nowise particular—not objecting to the fishy flavour of the wild fowl—their pots and kettles are sure to be well supplied."

"Under those circumstances I should not object to be a light-keeper," observed the Baron. "The household expenses must be small, as they have no butcher's bills to pay or taxes either."

"It is a somewhat solitary life," said the skipper. "Each man to his taste, I prefer sailing over the free ocean, with my stout galiot under my feet and plenty of sea room."

"Couldn't we stop and get some of the birds?" asked the Baron, who from habit was constantly thinking of the best way to supply his larder. "They would be a welcome addition to our sea-stock of provisions."

"The lighthouse-men would consider that we were poaching on their preserves," said the skipper; "besides which, if we were to go nearer than we now are, we should run the galiot ashore. See, we are already leaving the lighthouse astern, and are now clear of the river."

"So I perceive," groaned the Count, as the vessel had heeled over and began to pitch and tumble.

"Never fear, Count," said the skipper, in an encouraging tone; "we shall soon be going free, and the galiot will then only roll pleasantly from side to side, and assist to rock you to sleep when you turn in your bunk."

"I'd rather not be rocked to sleep in that fashion," said the Count. "Ever since I was a baby I have been able to sleep perfectly well in my bed or arm-chair after dinner without being rocked. Couldn't you manage to keep the galiot quiet, just to please me?"

"I could not keep her quiet to please the King of the Netherlands, or the Burgomaster of Amsterdam or Rotterdam; no, not if you paid ten times the sum you have for your passage-money," answered the skipper, in a gruff tone.

"Then I suppose that I must submit to my hard fate," groaned the Count. "Though I do wish—I cannot help wishing—that I had not come to sea; and I here register the firm resolution I now form, that of my own free will I will never —when once I set foot on shore—venture again on the stormy ocean."

"Then I must observe, my dear Count, that we shall never manage to get round the world, as you led me to suppose, when we started on our travels, it was your desire to do," observed the Baron.

"Yes, but I did not take into consideration that we should have to encounter so rough, ill-mannered, and boisterous a sea, and such howling winds," answered the Count. "I had bargained to find the water as smooth as the Scheldt, and I still should have no hesitation about going round the world, providing you can guarantee that the ocean will keep perfectly quiet till we come back again."

"As to that, I will guarantee that as far as my influence extends it shall remain as calm as a mill-pond," said the Baron, in a confident tone. "Will that satisfy you, Count? If so, notwithstanding your unjust complaints, we will continue our travels."

"Perfectly, perfectly," said the Count. "I always take your word for what it is worth."

"Hó! ho!" laughed the skipper, who overheard the conversation. "Look out there, Pieter. Are you keeping your weather eye open?" he shouted to the one-eyed mariner who was forward.

"Ja, ja, Captain; there's a fleet of fishing boats ahead, we must keep to the eastward of them. Port the helm a little."

Presently the Count and the Baron heard the tinkling of bells, and as they looked over the side of the vessel the Count exclaimed, "What are those Will-o'-the-Wisps dancing away there?"

"Ho! ho! ho!" laughed the skipper. "Those

are the lights from fishing boats. We shall see them more clearly presently."

As the galiot sailed on, the Count and Baron observed that the lights proceeded from lanterns hung up in the rigging, and that some vessels had huge beams with black nets attached to them

which they had just hoisted up out of the water, and that the crews were turning out the fish caught in the pockets of the nets. Others, under easy sail, were gliding on slowly with stout ropes towing astern.

"They are trawlers catching turbot, brill, plaice, and other flat fish," observed the skipper. " Our

country has numberless advantages; we make as
much use of the sea as many other nations do of
the land, though, as I before said, we are carrying on a constant warfare with it, trying to turn
it away from its ancient boundaries, and doing our
best to keep it from encroaching on the soil we
have once gained. Holland would never have become what she is, unless Dutchmen had been
imbued with a large quantity of those valuable
qualities, patience and perseverance."

"Ah, you Dutchmen are indeed a wonderful
people," exclaimed the Count. "I am very glad that
we thought of visiting your country before proceeding
to other parts of the world. At the same time,
if we had gone by land we should certainly have
seen more of it than we are likely to do now."

"Wait till daylight," said the skipper, "and
then you shall see what you shall see. I would
advise you to go below and obtain some sleep, as
at present, I will allow, the landscape is somewhat limited."

"You are right; the chief objects we can distinguish are the tip of your nose and Pieter's one eye, which I see blinking away when the light of the binnacle lamp falls on it," observed the Baron. "We will follow your advice," and he descended the companion-ladder.

The Count also commenced his descent into the cabin, but just before his head disappeared, he said: "You will oblige me greatly, Captain, by keeping the vessel as steady as you can; I find it very inconvenient to be tumbled and tossed about in the way we have been since we left the Maas."

"Ja, ja," answered the skipper, with a broad grin on his countenance, which, being dark, the Count did not observe.

CHAPTER IV.

OME on deck, Mynheers! come on deck!" cried the skipper, calling down the skylight. "The sun will soon rise, you can enjoy a sight of the land."

The Count and the Baron were soon dressed, and made their appearance on deck.

"There's the land, Mynheers, and you will soon see the sun rising from behind it," said the skipper, pointing with no little pride in his countenance to a long unbroken line of shore rising not many feet above the level of the ocean, with here and there a windmill towering above it; its arms just beginning to revolve as the morning breezes filled its sails. "There is Holland; look and admire."

While he was speaking, the sun, throwing a ruddy light on the dancing waves, rose behind the long line of coast and its countless windmills. The wind was fair, and the vessel was still steering northward.

" How soon are we likely to get into the Zuyder Zee ?" asked the Count.

" That depends on the continuance of the breeze," answered the skipper. " If it blows fair for a few hours more, we shall be up to the Helder before noon ; but if it shifts ahead, or a calm comes on, I shall have the pleasure of your company for some time longer."

"With due respect to you, Captain Jan Dunck, I sincerely hope that the breeze will continue fair," said the Count, making a polite bow, as he had no wish to offend the skipper, but felt constrained to speak the truth. " It is not of you or your galiot that I'm tired, but of this fidgetty sea which rolls and tumbles her about so thoughtlessly, to say the best of it."

" But are you aware, Count," said the skipper,

"that the Zuyder Zee can roll and tumble in no gentle fashion? For your sakes it is to be hoped that we shall not have a storm till you land safely in Amsterdam."

"Then I sincerely pray that the winds may be in a gentle mood," said the Count.

"And in the meantime, Captain Jan Dunck, I propose that we go down to breakfast," said the Baron, who had showed signs of impatience for some time past.

The Count and the Baron and the skipper sat down to breakfast. The two latter did ample justice to the good things placed before them; but the Count, after several heroic attempts to swallow a big sausage, had to confess that his appetite had vanished, and that he thought that the fresh air on deck would restore it. He there found the one-eyed mariner steering.

"Oh tell me, brave sailor, when are we likely to get to the Helder?" he asked in a tone which showed that he was but ill at ease.

"If you open your eyes wide enough, you will

see it right ahead," answered the one-eyed mariner. "That point of land out there, that's the Helder; we shall sail close to it, if the wind holds fair, and the tide does not sweep us out again. There's water enough there to float a seventy-four. On the other side is the island of Texel, and a very fine island it is for sheep; many thousands live on it; and if you wish to taste something excellent, I would advise you to obtain one of the green cheeses which are made from the milk of the sheep living on the island."

"I will tell the Baron, who thinks more of eating than I do," answered the Count. "But is that actually the Helder I see before me?"

"I told you it was," answered the one-eyed mariner, in a gruff tone, as if he did not like to have his word doubted.

This was indeed joyful news to the Count, who already began to feel his appetite returning; and he could not resist the temptation of shouting through the skylight to the Baron, inviting him to come up and see the place.

"Sit quiet till you have finished your breakfast, there will be time enough then, and to spare," observed the skipper, who knew very well that the tide was running out, and that the galiot could not stem it for some time to come.

In half-an-hour after this the galiot began to move ahead, and arrived off a huge sea wall, two hundred feet from the foundation to the summit, and built of Norwegian granite, a work constructed to protect the land from the encroachments of the ocean. Beyond it could be seen the tops of the houses and the steeples of a large town. Sailing on, the galiot came off the town of Nieuwe Diep, and the tall masts and yards of a number of large ships could be distinguished in the Royal Dockyard inside the bank.

"We Dutchmen are proud of this place," observed the skipper. "Two hundred years ago a fierce naval battle was fought off here between the English and French, and our brave Admirals De Ruyter and Van Tromp, who gained the victory."

After the galiot had passed Nieuwe Diep the

wind shifted to the northward, and she ran on
rapidly in smooth water till she came off Enkhuisen.
Rounding that point she reached Hoorn, off which
she brought up.

"The place is worth seeing," observed the
skipper; "and you may spend an hour or two on
shore while I transact some business. You will
remember that it was once the capital of North
Holland, but it is now what some people call a
dead city, and you will acknowledge that it is
very far from being a lively one; however, it has
something to boast of. It was here that Captain
Schouten was born—he who sailed with Le Maire
and discovered the southern end of America, to
which he, in consequence, gave the name of his
birthplace. You have heard of Cape Horn, I
suppose."

"Oh, yes; as to that, the Baron knows all
about it," said the Count. "We will follow your
advice, Captain, and will be down on the quay
again within the time you mention."

"Well, this is a dead city," said the Baron, as

HOORN.

he and the Count walked through its ancient streets. "Everything about it seems to indicate that if it ever were alive it must have been a long time ago. What curious old houses, how quaint in form; many of them also are decorated with sculpture of all sorts, and, on my word, excessively well executed too."

"I should be very unwilling to pass many days here," remarked the Count, as passing along street after street they scarcely met a creature, quadruped or biped. The houses seemed untenanted—not a voice, not a sound was heard; yet they were all clean, in good preservation, and well painted, mostly of a yellow colour with red roofs, many of them with gable ends, one story being smaller than the other, so that towards the summit they presented an outline of steps. There were also numerous gateways, some handsomely carved, but they led nowhere, and indeed no one was seen to go in or out at them.

"I cannot stand this," said the Count. "Let us go back to the port." Here a certain amount of trade was going on. Hoorn is engaged largely in the curing of herrings; some vessels also were building, and it was evident from the number of cheeses stacked up ready for exportation that it must carry on a considerable commerce in that article. Floors above floors were piled with round red cannon-balls, emitting an odour powerful if not pleasant.

"After all, Hoorn is not so dead as I supposed," observed the Baron.

Finding the skipper they embarked.

"You intend, I hope, to land us at Amsterdam to-night," said the Count to the skipper.

"Don't think there's the slightest chance of it," was the answer. "The wind has fallen, it will be stark calm in a few minutes; for what I can see it will be a calm all the night through and to-morrow also."

"Then I propose that we go to dinner," said the Baron. "I hope that it will be ready soon."

"Dinner is it you want?" exclaimed the skipper. "What, did you not dine at Hoorn?"

"Certainly not," said the Baron. "We were employed in seeing the town. We fully expected that you would have had dinner ready on our return on board. What has become of all the provisions you shipped, may I ask?"

"I landed them at Hoorn, where I took my own dinner," answered the skipper. "You must manage to rough it on bread and cheese. There's not much bread, but you may eat as much cheese as you like."

"This is abominable treatment, Captain Jan Dunck," exclaimed the Baron. "I insist that you obtain provisions at the first place you can reach, or else that you land us where we can obtain them. I am sure the Count agrees with me."

"Ho, ho, ho!" laughed the skipper. "Who do you think is master of this ship? Did you ever hear the old song?—

> 'Mynheer Jan Dunck,
> Though he never got drunk,
>   Sipped brandy and water gaily;
> He quenched his thirst
> With a quart of the first,
>   And a pint of the latter daily.'

That's just what I have been doing, although I'm as sober as a judge. I am ready for anything.

You want to be landed, do you? Suppose I put you on shore on the island of Marken? It is not far off, and my boat will carry you there. What then will you say for yourselves? It is your own doing, remember."

"This treatment is abominable," exclaimed the Baron. "I appeal to your crew for their assistance, and ask them if they will stand by and see your passengers insulted in this fashion."

"Ho, ho, ho!" laughed the skipper. "Hoist the boat out. We will soon see if my crew dare to disobey me. Pieter, there, be smart about it."

The one-eyed mariner started up and eyed the Count and the Baron with his single blinker, making a grimace as much as to say he could not help it. He and the mate and the small ship's boy soon got the boat into the water.

"Step in," cried the skipper. "You said you wanted to be put on shore, and I am going to put you on shore. Pieter, you're to row. If you want your dinners you'll embark, if not you'll go without them."

"And are you going too, Captain Jan Dunck?'
asked the Baron.

"Certainly, it is my intention," answered the
skipper, and the Count and the Baron, with their
valises, got into the boat.

"Look after the vessel," shouted the skipper to
the mate and small ship's boy, as he stepped into
the boat and seated himself in the stern sheets,
with the Count on one side and the Baron on the
other and Pieter pulling. As there was not a
breath of wind the water was perfectly smooth.
The Baron's hunger increased, the Count also had
regained his appetite, and they were eager to reach
the shore in the hopes of getting a dinner. The
skipper said nothing, but looked very glum. At last
the island appeared ahead, with a few huts on it
and a tiny church in the midst, but it was green
and pleasant to look at.

"That does not look like a place where we can
get dinner," observed the Baron, eyeing it doubtfully.

"And he does not intend to give you any dinner
either," whispered the one-eyed mariner, whose good-

will the Count and Baron had evidently won. " Take my advice, tell him to go up and obtain provisions, and say that you will eat them on board."

" What's that your talking about?" exclaimed the skipper. " Silence there, forward!"

The one-eyed mariner rowed slower and slower, and managed to carry on the conversation alternately with the Count and the Baron. Suddenly the skipper, who had been partly dozing, though he had managed to steer the boat, aroused himself. " Pull faster, Pieter," he shouted out: " I have heard what you have been talking about, and will pay you off."

" I was merely giving the gentlemen good advice, Captain," answered Pieter. " And there's one thing I have to say to you; if you can get provisions at Marken, you had better do so in a hurry, for there's a storm brewing, and it will be upon us before long. The mate and the boy won't be able to manage the galiot alone, and she to a certainty will be wrecked."

" A storm brewing, is there?" cried the Captain.

"Well, then, the sooner we land at Marken the better. Pull away, Pieter, pull away."

Pieter did pull, and in a short time the beach was reached. An old fisherman, with a pipe in his mouth and a red cap on his head, came down to see what the strangers wanted, as the Count and Baron stepped on shore.

" Friend," exclaimed the Baron, " can you tell us where a good dinner is to be obtained in a hurry, for we are famishing."

" A good dinner can undoubtedly be obtained in Marken," answered the ancient fisherman with the red nightcap on his head; " but we are not accus-, tomed to do things in a hurry in our island. Poultry have to be caught and their necks wrung, and the sheep have to be slaughtered and skinned and cut up, potatoes have to be dug, and the other vegetables gathered, the bread has to be made ; but we have cheese, and you can eat as much of that as you like."

" Plenty of cheese on board, we do not come on shore to obtain it !" exclaimed the Baron. " Captain

Jan Dunck, you have grossly deceived us; you brought us on shore with the expectation of speedily obtaining a good dinner."

"Ho, ho, ho!" laughed the skipper. "I said nothing of the sort; I undertook to land you, if you no longer wished to remain on board."

"But you led us to suppose that you intended to go yourself and obtain a fresh supply of provisions at Marken," said the Baron with emphasis; "and that is what we expected you to do."

"Then, Baron Stilkin, you are very much mistaken," answered the skipper. "You left my vessel of your own free will, and you have landed on this island of your own free will. I have fulfilled my engagement; if you want a dinner you must go and find it as best you can. I heard what Pieter was saying to you, and I intend to pay him off. Take up your portmanteaus, unless the old fisherman will carry them for you, and go your way; the storm, as Pieter observed, will be down upon us before long, and I must put off and return to the galiot."

"I again say that you are treating us shamefully!" exclaimed the Baron. "Pieter, my brave friend, will you stand by us?"

"Ja, ja, that I will," answered Pieter, who had stepped out of the boat. "If the Captain likes to go off, he may go by himself."

The discussion had been going on for some time when Pieter said this. Not only had the wind risen, but the rain had begun to fall, and the Count and Baron were preparing to put up their umbrellas.

"It is very fortunate we brought them," observed the Count. "Baron, your advice was sound when you suggested that we should do so."

Meantime the skipper had been getting his boat ready; he had stepped the mast, and hoisted the sail.

"Pieter!" he exclaimed, "I want to say something to you."

"What is it, Captain?" asked the one-eyed mariner, cautiously drawing near.

"Why, this!" cried the skipper. "That you are a treacherous old rascal, and that I intend to pay you off."

As he spoke he hove a noose at the end of a rope over Pieter's body, and before the one-eyed mariner was aware of what was going to happen, he was dragged off his feet into the water, while

the skipper, hauling aft the main-sheet, sailed away, dragging poor Pieter through the foaming waters astern. In his struggles Pieter had moved the rope up to his neck, and was now in danger of being throttled.

"Stop, stop!" shouted the Count and the Baron in chorus. "Let that man go! What are you about to do with him? You'll throttle him, or drag off his head, or drown him—you'll be guilty of murder. We'll report your conduct to the Burgomaster of Amsterdam, and all the other authorities of Holland. Release him, let him go!"

Captain Jan Dunck, who never looked back towards his victim, disregarding their threats and their cries sailed on, till he and his boat and the hapless Pieter disappeared amid the thick sheets of rain and the driving spray which surrounded them.

CHAPTER V.

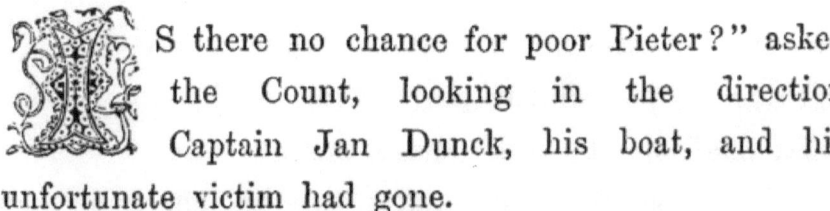S there no chance for poor Pieter?" asked the Count, looking in the direction Captain Jan Dunck, his boat, and his unfortunate victim had gone.

"None, unless the skipper relents and drags him on board; and then I don't think it likely that they will be on the best of terms," answered the Baron.

"Do Dutch skippers generally treat their crews in the way Captain Jan Dunck has treated poor Pieter?" asked the Count of the ancient fisherman.

"It depends very much on the amount of schiedam they have taken aboard," answered the ancient fisherman. "We of Marken do not behave in that fashion."

"I am very glad to hear it," said the Count, "as there seems a probability, till the storm is over, of our having to spend some time with you; if you were to do anything of the sort, we should undoubtedly report your conduct to the Burgomaster of Amsterdam, as we intend to report the conduct of Captain Jan Dunck, when we get there. And now, Baron, since it seems to be all up with the one-eyed mariner, and as at present we can do nothing to punish the perpetrator of the cruel deed, what shall we do with ourselves?"

"I propose that we request this ancient fisherman to conduct us to some hostelry, where we can obtain those creature comforts which we so much need, and wait in quiet and security till the storm is over. Worthy friend," he continued, turning to the ancient fisherman, "I beg that you will have the goodness to conduct us to some inn, where we may obtain a dinner and rest after our adventures on the stormy ocean."

"An inn," ejaculated the ancient fisherman. "We have no inns in Marken, as few travellers are in the habit of visiting us. If, however, you will accept such hospitality as I can offer, you shall be welcome to it."

"With all our hearts," answered the Count and the Baron in chorus, and they followed the ancient fisherman, who led the way into the interior of the island. After passing through several narrow and dirty lanes they emerged into a more open space, where they found themselves surrounded by neat cottages, among which a number of people were moving about.

The men were all dressed as sailors—a brown knitted vest and wide knickerbockers tied at the knees, thick black or blue woollen stockings, and wooden sabots or shoes. These sabots, the Count and the Baron observed, were taken off when the men entered a hut, so that it could be known how many people were inside by the number of sabots at the door. The women wore brown or chintz vests, and short dark petticoats; many of them had their hair hanging down on either side of the face in long thick curls; their head-dresses were high white caps rounded at the summit and lined with some coloured material.

"Here is my house," said the ancient fisherman,

opening the door of one of the neatest cottages in the place, "and there is my vrouw."

As he spoke an old lady got up and welcomed the travellers. She wore the dress which has been described, especially clean and picturesque, and in addition several gold ornaments. The cottage contained many marks of thrift; two carved oaken wardrobes stood one on either side, there was a clock of elaborate workmanship, and china plates of a curious pattern. A cheerful fire burned on the hearth, and the ancient fisherman's wife soon busied herself with her highly-polished pots and pans in preparing a meal, the very odour of which made the Baron's mouth water. Freshly-caught fish and a stew with potatoes and vegetables were quickly ready, and the Baron did ample justice to each dish placed on the table. The ancient fisherman informed them that the population of the island was about nine hundred; the men are all fishers, and pass the greater portion of their days on the water. On Sunday night, or rather as soon as Monday is commenced, the whole population go down to the port; the men embark in their boats, put to sea, and pass the week in fishing. The women return to their daily avocations till another Saturday afternoon comes round, when the men return home for their day of rest.

"Month after month, and year after year, we live the same style of life; the world wags on around us, but we hear little or nothing of its doings. We are contented and happy in our way, and wouldn't change our island of Marken for any part of the Netherlands, or the whole of Europe to boot," said the ancient fisherman.

"I am much inclined to stop among you," observed the Count. "Only I should not like to have to go out fishing every day, especially in cold and wintry weather; but to sit here, for instance, with one's feet before the fire, is very pleasant."

The ancient fisherman laughed. "You must remember, Mynheer, that in order to obtain these comforts, my father and I have toiled on year after year, each adding a little; this cottage and what it contains, represents the labour, I may say, of centuries. Few things worth having are to be obtained without working. I can enjoy my ease and these comforts with a clear conscience, for I have laboured on for fifty years or more, adding to the store my father left me, and he laboured for more than fifty years, and my grandfather before him."

"What examples you and your family are of patience and perseverance," observed the Count.

"No, Mynheer, nothing wonderful," answered the ancient fisherman, in a modest tone. "All the inhabitants of our part of the town have done much the same, and we bring up our children in the hope that they will follow our example. This, Mynheer, is the secret of our contentment and prosperity."

"Then, when I marry and have children, I must bring them up to follow my example, and the same result will, I hope, follow," said the Count.

"That depends upon the example you set them," answered the ancient fisherman.

"Ah, yes; I must see about it, then," said the Count. "I don't know that as yet I have ever done anything very industrious. Perhaps, like me, they will become great travellers."

"Perhaps, my dear Count, the less you say about it the better, at present," observed the Baron. "We have not proceeded very far on our voyage round the world. In the meantime, I will thank our hostess for another cup of her excellent tea."

As there seemed no probability of the storm abating, the Count and the Baron accepted the invitation given them by the ancient fisherman and his dame, to spend the night in their cottage. They had no beds to offer, but they had comfortable arm-chairs, pipes, tobacco, and a blazing fire.

"We might be worse off," observed the Baron, as he extended his legs and folded his arms to sleep.

It being impossible to reach the mainland without a boat, the Baron suggested, that after their experience, it would be safer to have one of their own than to entrust themselves again to strangers, and the Count agreeing, they settled to buy one. The next morning, therefore, after breakfast, having wished their ancient host and hostess farewell, and the Count having slipped a coin into the hand of the latter as a remembrance, they purchased a boat, which the ancient fisherman recommended, and helped them to launch: they then together set forth to prosecute their travels.

Neither of them were very expert navigators, though the ancient fisherman gave them a shove off to assist them in their progress, which was remarkably slow. Sometimes they rowed one way, and sometimes another, and the boat consequently went round and round.

"You pull too hard," cried the Count.

"You don't pull hard enough," answered the Baron. "That is the reason we don't go as straight as we should."

"Then perhaps if you take the two oars we shall go straighter," said the Count.

To this the Baron objected, as he had no desire to undertake all the labour of the voyage. Somehow or other they managed, notwithstanding, to get to a distance from Marken: perhaps the tide was carrying them along in the direction of the Helder; that this was the case, however, did not occur to them. They saw the land clearly enough stretching out to the westward: there lay Monnickendam, there Edam, and, further to the south, Uitdam. " Experience makes perfect :" after some time they did manage to row in a fashion.

" I think we must be approaching the shore," observed the Count. " It looks nearer than it did."

" So it ought, since we have been rowing with might and main for the last two hours," said the Baron, wiping the perspiration from his brow. " I wish that we had waited at Marken till we should have found a passage on board some vessel, or obtained the assistance of one of the islanders; this is heavy work, especially as we have come away without provisions."

" So we have," cried the Count. " Oh dear! oh dear! If we ever reach the shore, I shall be very much inclined to register a vow never again to tempt the stormy ocean."

" Regrets are useless at present; let us get to the shore," said the Baron.

But they rowed and rowed away in vain. Evening was approaching, and, though they had enjoyed a good breakfast, they were desperately hungry, and there appeared every probability that they would have to spend the night on the water. Fortunately it was calm, or they would have been in a still worse condition. Looking up, they at length saw an island, or a point of land with a tower on it.

"That must be one of the places on the coast," observed the Count; "let us try to reach it."

"But if we sit with our backs to the bows, as we have been hitherto doing, we shall not see it," observed the Baron. "Let us stand up and row forward; then, perhaps, we shall go straighter than we have been doing."

The Count agreed, and they rowed thus for some time.

Suddenly they were startled by a voice which in mournful accents said: "Oh, take me on board; take me on board!"

So great was the Baron's alarm that he nearly sank down to the bottom of the boat, when on

looking over his shoulder, what
should he see but the countenance
of the one-eyed mariner, who was
endeavouring to haul himself on
board.

"Are you yourself, or are you a ghost?" asked
the Baron, in trembling accents.

"Can it be? Can it be our former shipmate?" cried the Count.

"I am indeed, most noble gentlemen, that unfortunate and ill-used individual," answered the one-eyed mariner; for it was he himself, though his countenance was as pale as if he had really been a ghost, and his visage was elongated, the result of the sufferings he had gone through. Satisfied that he was a mortal being like themselves, the Count and the Baron at length assisted him to get into the boat.

"How did you escape?" asked the Baron eagerly.

"By a wonderful circumstance," answered the one-eyed mariner. "I managed to get my hands free, and slipped my neck out of the noose, just as I was on the point of being strangled. I held on to the boat, however, and allowed myself to be dragged along at the stern. I knew that if I had attempted to get in Captain Jan Dunck would very soon have quieted me by a blow on my crown. At length I saw that we were passing yonder island,

and, silently letting go the rope, I swam towards it; while he, unconscious of my escape, sailed on. I there landed, but it is a barren spot, where neither food nor fresh water is to be obtained. I thought that I should have perished; for after the strain on my throat I felt dreadfully thirsty, and capable of drinking up the Zuyder Zee itself, if it had been fresh water mixed with a due allowance of schiedam. At length I observed your boat, noble gentlemen, drifting by; I cannot compliment you by saying you were rowing, for you were going round and round in all directions. I guessed that you were land-lubbers—excuse my frankness—and that I might render you assistance in return for the service you would do me by enabling me to reach the shore. Not till you spoke, however, did I recognise you as my late shipmates, and now Mynheers, the best thing you can do is to let me take the oars and row steadily to the land; for, though hungry and thirsty, I have still some strength left in my battered frame."

"By all means, worthy mariner, take the oars,"

said the Baron, handing his to the sailor, while the Count followed his example. "We are ourselves nearly starving, and will promise you the best supper to be obtained wherever we may land, should we be fortunate enough to reach some hospitable part of the globe."

The one-eyed mariner took the oars, and bending lustily to them, made the boat move along very much faster than she had done since the Count and the Baron had commenced their voyage.

"I was inclined, when we were rowing, to suppose that she was among the slowest that ever floated, or that there was something the matter with the oars," observed the Count.

"People are very apt to find fault with the tools they employ, instead of laying the blame on themselves," remarked the Baron, sententiously.

The one-eyed mariner cocked his one eye, as much as to say, "You are right, gentlemen;" but without speaking he rowed and rowed, now bending forward, now leaning back with all his might, every now and then looking over his shoulder to see that they were

going in the right direction. It was getting darker
and darker, and no friendly lights beamed forth
from cottages or houses to indicate that they were
approaching the inhabited part of the country.

"Shall we soon reach the shore," asked the
Baron, with a groan; "I am getting desperately
hungry."

"We shall not get there the sooner by talking
about it," answered the one-eyed mariner, who was
beginning to lose his temper as he became more
and more fatigued. "If you, Mynheers, had learned
to row, you might have relieved me for a short
time, till I had recovered my strength; but as we
should never get there if I gave you up the oars,
I must keep at it; only do not be continually
asking me when we shall get there. I tell you
we shall get there, wherever that may be, some
time or other, if I keep rowing long enough."

After this remark, the Count and the Baron
thought it prudent to say nothing more to the
one-eyed mariner. He rowed and he rowed. The
land became more distinct, but no lights indicated

the cheerful habitations of men. The Baron groaned, for he saw no prospect of obtaining a supper, yet it was better to be on dry land than in a small boat on the Zuyder Zee, with an individual of so uncertain a temper as the one-eyed mariner. At length they found themselves with banks on either side.

"I thought so," said the one-eyed mariner, "we have reached the neighbourhood of Yollendam; this must be the Yoll—a better landfall than I expected. I do not know that provisions are to be obtained at the village, which is a mile or so off; but we will see. And he rowed up the river, which had a more attractive appearance than might have been expected, for there was a small island covered with trees, and a mound several feet high on the opposite side, on which the eye could rest with pleasure. Before they had gone far the moon burst forth from behind some clouds, and shed along the waters of the stream its silvery light, which showed them a small vessel drawn up on the shore, and two or three people near her.

" Perhaps these per-
sons have provisions
on board," exclaimed
the Baron. " I could
sup off a dry crust of
bread and a piece of
Dutch cheese with greatest willingness in the world.
We will ask those strangers if they will kindly relieve
our necessities.   Brave sailor, good Pieter, old and

worthy shipmate, have the goodness to pull in for the shore, and we will throw ourselves on the charity of those strangers."

The one-eyed mariner gave a grunt, as if he valued but little the compliments paid him; but he obeyed, notwithstanding, and the boat soon reached the shore. The Baron and the Count then scrambled out, and made their way to where the crew of the vessel were seated.

"Worthy mariners," began the Baron, in his usual style; "we are shipwrecked individuals, or rather, I should say, we have just come a long and perilous voyage in yonder small boat, without food or liquid with which to renew our strength, and we are well-nigh starving. We ask you forthwith to supply our necessities."

"What's the stout gentleman talking about?" asked one of the sailors of his companion. "I cannot make out what he says."

"So far as I can understand, he and his friend are hungry, and want some grub," observed the latter. "Food is it you want?" he continued, turning to the Count and the Baron. "Our vessel there, which we hope to get off at high tide, is laden with cheese, and you shall have one apiece if you like at cost price, with as much biscuit as you can eat and some schnapps into the bargain."

"By all means, let us go on board at once," cried the Baron. "I am grateful to you."

"But we must not forget poor Pieter," cried the Count. "Here Pieter, Pieter, we have got some food for you."

Pieter had hauled up the boat, and, moving as fast as he could stagger, he accompanied the Count and the Baron and the crew of the sloop on board. The sailors were as good as their word, and produced a couple of round ruddy cheeses and a basketful of biscuits.

"Let us attack one first," said the Baron, nearly breaking his knife in the attempt to make an incision in the rind; he succeeded in getting off some slices, and all three fell to. Pieter, who was the most hungry of the party, swallowed one huge lump after another, then held out his cup for a supply of schiedam.

"Never mind the water," he observed. "This dry biscuit and cheese requires something potent to get it down."

The Count, who had never tasted schiedam before, though he took his diluted with water, made wry faces at what he considered its nauseous taste, but he said nothing for fear of offending the captain and crew of the sloop. At length he declared that he could eat no more.

"I think I can go on a little longer," said the Baron, who had attacked the second cheese.

"And I do not expect to leave off till midnight," said the one-eyed mariner, helping himself to an additional slice. At last their meal came to a conclusion.

"Where are you bound for?" asked the Count of the skipper of the sloop.

"For Amsterdam," answered the skipper.

"Then, Baron, don't you think that it would be as well if we were to proceed on board this vessel, supposing the captain is willing to give us a passage?" said the Count.

"As to that, we might do worse," answered the Baron. "We shall thus at all events accomplish our passage to Amsterdam by water as we intended, and the Zuyder Zee is not likely to prove as boisterous as the Northern Ocean."

The skipper of the sloop having no objection to take the Count and the Baron, the arrangement was at once concluded.

"By-the-by, my friend," said the Baron, "I hope you will manage to obtain some more nutritious and palatable provender than these red cheeses and hard biscuit for the voyage: they are all very well once in a way for supper, but I should not like to have nothing else to live on."

The skipper promised to send to Yollendam, or if not to Edam, to obtain provisions for his passengers.

"And pray, Mynheers, what are you going to do with your boat," asked the one-eyed mariner.

"I forgot all about her," exclaimed the Count.

"We will present her to you, my worthy friend," he said. "You shall become her skipper, and, if you please, you are welcome to sail round the world in her, provided we are not compelled to accompany you."

The one-eyed mariner gratefully accepted the gift. "I am a made man," he said, "and need no longer be at the beck and call of Captain Jan Dunck, supposing he and the *Golden Hog* are still afloat. I will obtain fishing lines, and go out and fish and sell my fish, and build a cottage, and marry a wife, and live happy and independent to the end of my days."

A bright idea seemed to strike the Count. "Friend, if you happen not to have found a wife in these parts, pray come over to Belgium, and I will there introduce you to a charming person, Johanna Klack by name, and you can take her away with you and settle at Marken or Urk, or any other island in or about the Zuyder Zee."

"Excellent! the brightest idea, my dear Count, to which you ever gave birth," exclaimed the

Baron. " By all means, worthy Pieter, come. Don't trouble yourself to look out for a wife here ; they're all very good in their way, but Johanna Klack is super-excellent, and she probably has saved up a whole stockingful of guilders. I feel very much inclined to go back with you at once to assist you in your wooing."

" Mynheer," said the one-eyed mariner, putting his finger to his nose, " ' good wine needs no bush.' I have an idea or two. If this dame is so very charming, somebody with more personal attractions than I possess will have won her before I have the happiness of making her acquaintance ; and you forget that, though I have got the boat, I have to obtain the fishing lines to catch the fish, to sell the fish, to go on doing that for some years, and then to build the house, and when the house is built it will be time enough for me to come in search of Vrouw Johanna Klack."

" Well, well, we'll talk about that to-morrow morning," said the Baron, who did not feel very sanguine as to the speedy disposal of Johanna Klack's fair hand.

Pieter, wishing them good night, went to sleep on board his boat, while they turned into two bunks in the small cabin of the sloop and slept soundly.

CHAPTER VI.

WHEN the Count and the Baron awoke, they found to their surprise that the sloop was not only afloat but under weigh, and sailing over the waters of the Zuyder Zee. The skipper, who was short and broad, had a crew of two men, who were, he assured his passengers, amply sufficient for navigating the sloop.

"We shall not reach Amsterdam quite as soon as you might have expected, Mynheers," he said; "for I purpose putting in at Monnickendam for a few hours. It is not a very lively place, though it was once a wealthy city, one of the twenty great towns of Holland, but its glory has passed away."

As the object of the Count and the Baron was

to see the world, they willingly agreed to visit this dead city of the Zuyder Zee. They were accordingly rowed on shore in the sloop's boat.

"Well, this does seem to be a city of the dead, or else the inhabitants, if there are any, have gone to sleep," observed the Baron, as he and the Count paced the streets, which were paved with yellow bricks. The houses were all red, and the venetian shutters green — one house was almost exactly like another; not a door nor a window was open, not a face was to be seen at any of them; through the entire length of one long thoroughfare they met not a single person—not a cat, nor a dog, nor a sign of life. They went through street after street—every street was the same; only when they returned to the harbour a few people collected to inspect them, examining minutely their boots and hats, their coats and umbrellas.

"Well, gentlemen," said the Baron, making them a profound bow, "you will remember us should we ever have the pleasure of paying your defunct city another visit."

He and the Count stepped into the boat which was waiting to take them on board the sloop. Whatever other business the skipper transacted at Monnickendam, he had not omitted to imbibe a considerable amount of schiedam, and although when he stepped on deck he was as steady as a church steeple, there was a twinkle in his eye, and a mode of expressing himself which showed what he had been about. The Count and the Baron, however, did not at first discover this. When the sloop was got under weigh, he invited them into the cabin to partake of the dinner, which one of the crew had prepared. The wind was light, and the sloop glided steadily on.

"After all, I really do think I like the sea," said the Count. "This style of navigation suits me— no trouble, no fatigue. We can eat and drink and go to sleep, and return on deck to enjoy the fresh air. When, Captain, do you think we shall reach Rotterdam?"

"Reach Rotterdam, Mynheers, why when the sloop gets there," answered the skipper. "I cannot say how soon we shall reach it, the winds must know more about that than I do. We have Uitdam and Durgerdam to pass first, and the wind may fail us or become contrary. It was not in our agreement to tell you when we should get there; have patience, Mynheers, have patience; let the world go round as it likes, and have patience."

This was not a very satisfactory answer, but as the Count and the Baron were tolerably comfortable they made no complaint. The skipper sat in his chair, and after he had finished dinner quaffed schiedam and water; one of the crew was engaged below in cleaning up the dishes and plates, the other was at the helm. Presently there came a loud cry, and the cutter heeled over. The Count, who was the most active of the party, jumped up to see what was the matter, while the man forward did the same.

" We're run into by a big, lubberly ship," cried the man at the helm.

The fact was very clear. The bowsprit of the big ship had caught the rigging of the sloop, and was bearing her over.

"What is going to happen?" asked the Count, in a state of no small trepidation.

"We shall be sent to the bottom if our mast and rigging are not carried away," answered the man at the helm.

The crew of the big ship were rushing out to

the bowsprit end to try and clear the sloop, but that seemed no easy matter.

"Can't you cut the rigging, my friends?" shouted the Count, who at a glance saw that by so doing the sloop would be set free.

"But we shall lose our mast if they do that," said the man at the helm.

"Better lose our mast than be sent to the bottom," answered the Count.

Again he shouted, "Cut, my friends, cut."

The sailor who had sprung to the end of the jibboom, supposing the Count to be the captain, did as he was bid, and with a few strokes of an axe quickly severed the rigging, and the shrouds fell down on deck, while the sloop, gliding on, was quickly free of the ship.

"Why didn't you keep a better look-out?" shouted the captain of the ship. "It was your own fault in getting in our way."

"Ja, ja," answered the man at the helm, who like the skipper had been indulging in potations of schiedam. The skipper himself now came on deck,

to which the Baron had just before made his way,
and began storming and raging. The crew of the
big ship only laughed at him and sailed proudly
on, while the sloop lay helpless on the water.

"The sooner we repair the rigging the better,"
observed the Count, who never put himself out,
whatever happened. The only man who was capable
of doing this was the one who had been forward;
he at once lowered down the mainsail and saved
the mast from being carried away, which it might
have been had a slight puff of wind come on.

"Put the vessel to rights, you lubbers," cried
the skipper. "I am going below to finish my
bottle of schiedam."

"Ja, ja," answered the sober man of the crew.
"Mynheers, will you help me, and we shall be
able to do it," he said, addressing the Count and
the Baron.

They consented to do their best to pull and
haul as much as was required.

"That's all I want," he said, fixing a rope to
the severed rigging and going aloft with it. Having

passed it through a block he told them to haul away. When the upper end had reached the masthead he lashed it there as securely as he could.

"That will do, provided we do not get a strong breeze. Now, Mynheers, help me to set the mainsail."

The Count and the Baron hauled away right lustily, and the sail was soon set.

"Now," said the sober sailor to the man who had been at the helm, "go forward and sleep; it is the only thing you're fit for at present."

The seaman obeyed, and disappeared down the fore hatchway. The sloop sailed on and on. The Count looked into the cabin and saw that the skipper was fast asleep; the Baron went forward and found half his crew employed in the same way.

"Never mind," said the sober sailor; "the wind is fair, and provided no other big ship runs us down we shall get safely to Amsterdam soon after nightfall."

This was cheering news to the travellers, and they promised a handsome reward to the sober sailor if he would take them in safely.

"Glad to do that for my own sake," he answered. "It won't be my fault if we do not."

Still, as the wind was light the sloop sailed slowly; yet it was very evident, from the number of vessels they encountered, that they were approaching the great emporium of commerce; but the evening was drawing on, and darkness would increase the dangers of the voyage. At length they could only see lights glittering here and there, ahead and on every side, and tall masts rising out of the water. Now and then shouts warned them to get out of the way of some vessel, and the sober sailor shouted in return.

"Now, Mynheers, whichever of you can steer the best take the helm, and we will bring the sloop to an anchor. We must wait till daylight to get through the outer drawbridge."

"I never steered in my life," answered the Count.

"Nor I either," said the Baron.

"Then do one of you take the tiller and do as I tell you," said the sober sailor.

"Baron, I leave that honour to you," said the Count; "I do not feel quite up to it."

The Baron, who would have been ready to steer a seventy-four if he had been asked, at once took the tiller in hand, and, as the sailor sang out, "Pull the tiller towards you," or "Put it away from you," he did as he was bid. They glided on in the darkness, the lights round them twinkling like fireflies. At last the sailor hauled down the jib and foresail. "Now put it from you," he sang out, "as far as you can." Then there came a splash, and the cable ran out, and the sober sailor requested the Count and the Baron to help him lower the mainsail.

"Now I have you all snug," he said, "I can put you on shore, or you can remain on board till morning if you wish it."

"I think we had better remain on board," said the Baron; "I do not fancy going into a strange town at midnight without knowing an inch of my way, or what hotel to go to."

"I agree with you," observed the Count, "though I cannot say that I anticipate much pleasure in passing the night in a close cabin with a tipsy skipper snoring as loud as a grampus.

"Not pleasant, certainly," remarked the Baron; "and I am ready to sacrifice myself for your benefit, if our friend here will take me on shore and wait for me while I search for an hotel; whether I find one or not, I will come back to you."

The Count gladly agreed to this proposal; and the sober sailor, launching the boat, at once put off with the Baron, intending, as he said, to land him at a quay at no great distance. The Count walked the deck impatiently waiting his return; and, as he heard the skipper and the man forward snoring, he began to regret that he had not himself also gone. The sober sailor and the Baron were a long time absent.

"What can have become of them?" exclaimed the Count, over and over again. He had sat down to rest in the after part of the vessel, when he saw some one moving forward; and, going in that direction, he discovered the sailor who had been asleep.

"What are you about there?" he asked.

"Giving more scope to the cable," was the

answer. "The tide has risen, and the sloop wants it."

"All right, I suppose," thought the Count, and he went aft, while the sailor descended, and was soon again fast asleep. The Count heard a noise such as rope makes when running over wood. Presently he observed that the objects, dimly seen through the gloom of night, were moving. "What can have happened?" he thought. Faster and faster they moved. The vessel appeared to be in a rapid current.

"Oh, dear! oh, dear! what is happening?" he cried out; and he shouted to the skipper and the man forward, but neither answered him. Presently the vessel struck against the side of a house which rose out of the water, then against a pier, then she bounded off, then once more she came with tremendous force against another house, which appeared to be a store, carrying away her bowsprit. "She will go to the bottom, and I shall be drowned," thought the Count; and he scrambled up the rigging just as the head of the mast poked its way in at a large opening in the wall. Climbing the shrouds of a vessel was a feat the Count had never before accomplished, and was very contrary to his habits; but he exerted himself to the utmost. The unpleasant recollection came upon him, as he was doing so, that

these were the shrouds which had been severed when
the ship ran into the sloop, and he feared, naturally,
that they would give way at the very moment that
he was upon them. This made him climb the faster.
Now, as the vessel heeled over, his feet touched the
wall of the building, and he feared that he might be
jammed against it. The darkness prevented him
from seeing clearly what was befalling the hull, but
his impression was that it was going down into the
deep canal, and that the skipper and the remaining
portion of his crew would be drowned; but he had
no desire to share their fate, and was utterly unable
to help them. He shouted, however, loud enough
to arouse them out of any ordinary slumber; but
the schiedam they had drunk had so completely
lulled their senses that they heard not his shouts,
or the bumping of the vessel against the wall. He
therefore continued his ascent till he reached the
top of the mast, when, getting hold of a beam
which projected from the opening in the building,
he hauled himself up. Just as he did so the mast
cracked; the vessel with a jerk heeled over to the

opposite side; he was left clinging to the beam while she was borne away by the tide into the darkness. Again he shouted to try and arouse the skipper, but no human voice replied to his cries.

CHAPTER VII.

THE Count felt about with his feet till they touched the floor of the loft into which he had scrambled. "Here I am landed at last, at all events," he said to himself; "but this, though dry enough, is not a pleasant place in which to pass the night ; and besides, my friend Stilkin will be searching for me, and be very much alarmed at not finding the vessel, or if he does find her—supposing she has not gone to the bottom—when he discovers that I have absconded. What can I do? I must try and get down into the street, and then, perhaps, I shall meet him and relieve his anxiety. I wish that I had a light, though, as I shall run the risk of tumbling down some trap-door and breaking my neck. I must move cautiously. This appears to be a lumber loft of some sort; it cannot contain valuable merchandise, or the opening through which I made an entrance would have been closed. Well, I am of opinion that this is the least pleasant of my adventures." The Count stopped. Looking back, he observed the outline of an opening through which came a small amount of light—such light as exists at night. This assisted him to direct his course across the floor of the loft: he moved cautiously, for every moment he knocked his feet against pieces of plank, and broken chests, and casks, and heaps of old sails, and fragments of rope piled up to be turned into oakum, and broken chains, and scraps of iron, and worn-out brooms and brushes. "I suppose there is an outlet somewhere, though I cannot yet distinguish it," he said to himself. "These things have probably been brought up from below; but suppose they have been only hoisted in through the window, I shall be imprisoned as effectually as if I had been shut in by bars and bolts, for I certainly cannot make my

escape through the opening by which I entered;
I should only fall into the canal. Dear me! dear
me! this is unpleasant. I wish that I had stayed
at home in my old castle. However, wishes are
vain things. I must try to get out somehow or
other." Again he began to grope about, feeling
with his hands and feet, but in spite of all efforts
could discover no outlet. "Probably, after all, it
will be wiser to sit down and wait till daylight,"
he thought. He accordingly sat himself down on
a pile of rope, but he had not sat there long before
he heard strange noises, a clattering and clamber-
ing of some creatures or other, and presently two
or three came bounding over his feet.

"Those must be rats," he said to himself. "I
have heard of a species which comes from Norway,
great savage creatures, a few dozen of which would
eat up a man at a meal; if I go to sleep they
may eat me up, and that will be objectionable in
the highest degree. It is very clear that I must
get out of this if I wish to keep a whole skin in
my body. Come! arouse thee, brave Funnibos! let

it not be said that the last of thy race was eaten up by rats."

He once more got up and resumed his search; as he was feeling about his hands struck against a large ring: " This perhaps is a trap-door," he thought.   Standing on one side, he pulled with all his might; it yielded, and he found that he was lifting it up.

" Yes, this is a trap-door, and the means of escape presents itself, but I must take care that there is a ladder by which to descend, or I may pitch down head foremost and crack my skull." Stooping over, he discovered to his satisfaction that there was a ladder, and he accordingly descended, holding on very tight with his hands, while he felt with his feet.   At last he reached the bottom, and found himself on a lower story; the windows, how- ever, if there were any, were closed.   He was not much better off than he had been on the story above; still, having succeeded thus far, he was determined not to be defeated, and again he began to search about.   The chamber appeared to have but little in it; now and then he knocked against a chest or a box, and stumbled over other articles, till suddenly he nearly fell head foremost down a stair. "This must lead somewhere, at all events," he thought; and by a banister which he discovered on one side he began cautiously to descend, feeling with one foot before he lifted up the other. Down and down he went till he got into a passage between some stone walls. "Come, perhaps this will conduct me to the street, or to the street door, and, if it is only closed with bolts and bars, I may withdraw them and set myself free. I only hope that there may be no inhabitants who may take me for a burglar, and shoot me before I have time to explain matters. I must go cautiously, so as to make no noise." He was going on feeling the walls on both sides, and putting one foot slowly before the other, when he observed a faint light streaming up from an opening on one side. The opening was a doorway; as he reached it the light became stronger, and he saw some stone steps leading to yet a lower story.

"This seems strange," he muttered, "I understood that the houses in Amsterdam were built on piles to keep them out of the water, and I should have supposed that a flight of steps so low as this would lead one into it ; but there must be some one down there, or this bright light would not be coming up.   Perhaps I had better go back to try and find my way to the street door, as I had intended, lest that somebody should consider that I am intruding; however, having got thus far, I will try and solve the mystery."   He, therefore, again descended step by step.   He found himself in a small vaulted chamber, in the centre of which was a table covered with retorts, jars, glasses of all shapes and sizes, and other chemical apparatus, while at a chair was seated a tall, grey-headed old gentleman, stirring the contents of a clay bowl with a glass tube; his eyes were so intently fixed on the bowl that he did not discover the presence of a stranger.   A lamp burning on the table shed the light around on the wizen countenance of the aged alchemist, on the walls of the chamber, and on the roof, from which hung suspended several iron chains, and stuffed birds and beasts and other creatures of curious form, unlike anything the Count had before seen. He stood for some time watching the proceedings of the unknown alchemist and considering what he should do; at last he gave a cough to attract attention. The old man looked up, and regarded him with a fixed stare.

"Who are you, and whence do you come?" he asked in a hollow voice. "Are you a spirit from the vasty deep, or have you risen from the nether world?"

"Though I am not a spirit, I have come from the vasty deep, for I am a shipwrecked traveller," answered the Count. "In a most extraordinary manner I was landed in a loft above this building, and have found my way down here. My object at present is to get out into the street of Amsterdam, for I presume I am in that city, and to discover my friend and companion, Baron Stilkin, who had, fortunately for himself, gone on shore before the catastrophe occurred, which nearly cost me my life;

and I shall be very, very much obliged to you, most reverend Seignor, if you will show me the door."

"At present I cannot on any account do that," answered the alchemist. "It might prove the destruction of my hopes were I to leave this crucible for a moment. Know that I am on the point of making the great discovery which is the object of my life," and the old man went on stirring as before.

"What is that discovery, may I ask?" inquired the Count.

"The means of converting tin into silver, and copper into gold; or rather, I may say, the discovery of the philosopher's stone, for which the sages of past centuries have searched in vain, but which I firmly believe it has been reserved for me to find out. I shall then become the richest individual in Amsterdam, and I have resolved to employ my wealth in rebuilding the city. I purpose to lay the foundations with granite instead of wooden piles, on which it now stands; to increase the width and depth of its canals, and double their present dimensions; to erect a church in the centre which shall surpass that of St. Peter's or St. Paul's; to make the inhabitants the most wealthy and healthy, the best and most contented people on the face of the globe. These are grand designs, you will allow, most noble stranger, for I perceive you are capable of appreciating them: these are sufficient to induce a man to burn the midnight oil, to spend his days in ceaselessly labouring at his allotted task."

"Perhaps you will be good enough to make haste and discover this philosopher's stone, and then let me out at your street door; for I am desperately hungry, and wish to find a hotel where I may obtain a supper and bed, in case I should not meet with Baron Stilkin, who landed for the express purpose of looking for one."

"Wait a few moments longer, my friend," said the alchemist, still stirring on. "You would not surely have me throw away the labour of years to gratify your selfish object. Just step aside in the meantime into that recess, as I am not quite certain what is about to happen. There may come an explosion, such has occurred before now, and then at the bottom of this crucible I firmly believe that I shall discover the philosopher's stone. It has never appeared yet, but, once in my possession, I shall leave this cold vault for ever, and emerge into the upper world, to commence the great undertaking I have designed. Stand aside! stand aside! at any moment there may be an explosion."

The Count at first thought that the wisest plan would be to escape up the stone steps, as he had no wish to be exposed to the effects of the expected explosion; but, curious to see the result, he stepped aside, as the old alchemist advised him, into a recess of the vault. Still the alchemist stirred on, but nothing occurred. The Count was losing patience when he heard the sound of feet descending the steps.

"Here comes my familiar spirit," muttered the alchemist; "he always does come just when I am about to make my grand discovery."

"He treads very heavily for a spirit!" thought the Count.

At that moment a remarkable and unattractive-looking person came into the light of the lamp; he was a short, thick-set man, with a huge head, almost a dwarf, dressed in a long coat and high boots, carrying in his hand a kettle.

The alchemist as he saw him started up. "Why have you come? Why hast thou come, thou enemy of science? thou who, night after night, hast prevented me from making the grand discovery, the aim of my existence, thou disturber of my studies, thou foe of the human race!"

"You know well enough, Mynheer Bosch, that what you say is all nonsense, and that I will not allow you to abuse me in this fashion," exclaimed the dwarf, lifting up the kettle as if he were about to throw it at the philosopher's head. "Come along, and leave your old bottles and jars; it is high time that you were in bed, and my business is to see you safe there, and to lock you up till to-morrow morning."

"But I have a visitor," said the philosopher, calming down, and looking perfectly resigned to his

fate. "A visitor who
may become my pupil,
and aid me in making
my grand discovery,
which has, through
your interference, been so long delayed."

"Any one who desires to become your pupil

must be a remarkably silly fellow," observed the dwarf. "If he is there, let him show himself. Come out, whoever you are, and I'll know how you ventured into this house without leave."

The Count, on hearing this, stepped forth from his hiding-place. "Honest man, pray understand, in the first place, that I have no desire to become. the pupil of this philosophical gentleman, that I most unintentionally entered the house, and shall be extremely obliged to you if you will let me out as soon as possible," he said; and he briefly explained how he had happened to get into the loft.

"That being the case, as soon as I have secured this poor old man for the night, I will show you out into the street," answered the dwarf; and taking hold of the lamp with one hand and with the other grasping the arm of the philosopher, who moved on as meekly as a lamb, he led the way up the steps, the Count following close behind. After proceeding along several passages he reached a door, when, producing a key from his pocket, he opened it.

"Go in," he said to the philosopher, "and wait

till I come back." The latter obeyed, and the dwarf locked him in.

"Now, Mynheer," he said, "having disposed of that poor old fellow for the present, I will show you the way out into the street; but take care you do not fall into the canal. You will not find any hotel in this part of the town fit for a gentleman of your rank; but if you go on straight before you and then turn to the right, then to the left, then to the right again, you may possibly meet with your friend whom you desire to find; if not, a watchman will take charge of you, should he not lock you up, and will help you to find an hotel."

This was not altogether satisfactory, for the Count doubted very much whether he should be able to follow the directions he had received; but he wanted to get into the open air, and he hoped that he should somehow or other find his way. He was not in the best possible mood, and had little expectation of finding the Baron; he was desperately hungry, and was afraid that his port-

K

manteau was lost, which would certainly be the
case if the sloop had gone to the bottom. However, finding himself in the open air, he went
along what appeared to be a narrow road, with
houses on one side and a canal on the other. The
odour which rose from the latter in the night air
was far from pleasant, but he soon got accustomed to it. He was inclined to shout out the
Baron's name as he went along, but it occurred to
him that some of the watchers of the night might
accuse him of being a disorderly person, and carry
him off to prison, though whenever he saw anyone
approaching he asked in a subdued tone, "Is that
you, Baron Stilkin?" But no one acknowledged
himself to be the Baron. Thus the Count went
on, no one impeding his progress. According to the
dwarf's advice, he did turn to the left and then to
the right, then to the left again, and turned
several times, till he forgot how many times he
had turned or where he was. For a long time he
met no one of whom to inquire the way. At last
he heard footsteps approaching. "Is that you,

Baron Stilkin?" he asked, as he had done before.

"What, whose voice is that?" exclaimed some one.

The Count, hoping that it was the Baron, replied, "Count Funnibos."

"What, my dear Count, is it you yourself?" exclaimed Baron Stilkin, for he it was, and, rushing into each other's arms, they wept, overcome by their feelings. The Count narrated the extraordinary adventures he had met with.

"And what about our portmanteaus and umbrellas? what will become of them?" exclaimed the Baron.

"They are on board the sloop, and, for what I can tell, at the bottom of the Zuyder Zee," said the Count.

"We must endeavour to regain them forthwith if they are afloat, or fish them up if they are at the bottom," said the Baron. "Come along. I left the sober sailor waiting for me. We may possibly find him, and at once put off in search of our property."

"But I should prefer having some supper first," exclaimed the Count. "I am well-nigh starving."

"Never mind, my dear Count," said the Baron, "I have eaten enough for two, and there's no time to be lost. It is of the greatest importance that we should forthwith recover our portmanteaus and umbrellas. Why, we have all the money in them, and our note-books and journals."

"And my ties and tooth-brush," put in the Count. "Of course, of course. I will still the cravings of my appetite and sacrifice my feelings for the common weal."

"Right, right; a noble principle," said the Baron. "I shall be able to enjoy a second supper with you when we return." And the Baron acting as guide, they set off for the quay where, to the best of his belief, he had left the sober sailor. Wonderful to relate, the sober sailor was there, waiting patiently, smoking his pipe with his arms folded, a picture of resignation. As far as could be perceived in the gloom of night, he did not appear to be much surprised at hearing of the accident which had befallen the sloop.

"Cheer up, Mynheers, we will find her," he said.

"She's not likely to have got far. There's a bit of a current round that point, but after that the tide runs slowly, and she will have been brought up by some other vessel across which she's been driven, or is still floating slowly out towards the Zuyder Zee." Saying this, he bent to his oars and pulled away down the canal. The lights glittered from the upper windows of many houses, showing that the inhabitants were not yet in bed, and the tall masts of numerous vessels towered up towards the sky, with yards across seen indistinctly in the gloom of night. The moon shone forth and shed her pale light on the smooth surface of the water, which looked bright and silvery, very different to the hue it is apt to wear in the daytime.

"If I were not so hungry and so anxious about our portmanteaus and umbrellas I should enjoy this," observed the Count.

"I do enjoy it," said the Baron, stroking his waistcoat. "As to our portmanteaus and umbrellas, my mind is greatly relieved by the assurances of our friend the sober sailor here."

"I hope you are so with sufficient reason," observed the Count, who was in low spirits, as people often are when they are hungry.

"I told you so, I told you so; there's the sloop," shouted the Baron. "I am right, am I not, friend mariner?"

"Ja, ja, that's she," answered the sober sailor, pulling towards the sloop, which was, as he had asserted would be the case, floating leisurely along, like a snail on a garden path. He soon pulled up alongside, when the Count and the Baron scrambled on board. The tipsy skipper and his tipsy crew were still both fast asleep in their respective bunks.

"Now I consider that it would be right and proper to let them float on after we have recovered our portmanteaus and umbrellas," said the Baron.

"It would be more kind and charitable to anchor the sloop, or to take her alongside the nearest vessel we can reach," said the Count. "What do you say, worthy mariner?"

"We cannot anchor her, because my messmate

slipped her cable and left the anchor in the canal,"
answered the sober sailor. "But we will tow her
alongside another vessel and make her fast, where
she will remain safe enough till I have conveyed
you, Mynheers, and your luggage to the shore. We
sailors make it a point of honour to look after our
shipmates when they get overtaken by too abundant
potations of schiedam or any other liquor."

"But you do not mean to say that you ever get
overtaken?" asked the Count.

"Not unless it is my turn to enjoy that
pleasure," answered the sober sailor. "It was my
turn to-night to keep sober, as it would never do
for the whole crew to get drunk together." Having
said this, the sober sailor stepped into the boat,
and towed the sloop up to a vessel which lay
conveniently near. Having secured her, and informed her skipper and crew of the condition of
his skipper and crew, he pulled away up to the
landing-place, carrying the Count and Baron, with
their portmanteaus and umbrellas. They were not
long, after landing, in finding a hotel, on entering

which the first words the Baron uttered were, "Supper for two."

"I thought that you had supped," remarked the Count.

"My dear Count, do you think I should be so uncourteous as not to eat a second to keep you company?" said the Baron, smiling blandly. They were soon seated at table, and the Baron did ample justice to his second supper.

CHAPTER VIII.

"THEN here we are in Amsterdam," said the Count to the Baron, as they sauntered out of their hotel after breakfast. "I wonder whether all these people have come to do us honour on hearing of our arrival."

"They probably have not heard of our arrival," said the Baron. "They are, as you will perceive, market people, and others who have come in these boats surrounding the landing-slips;" and he pointed across the crowd which thronged the quay to the canal, on which boats of various sizes were coming and going, mostly laden with cheeses and other merchandise to supply the city of Amsterdam.

"Ah, yes; you are probably correct," remarked

the   Count.
"Now let us set
forth and inspect this great city."

A guide, who had noticed them leaving the hotel,
offered his services to conduct them through the

streets, and to give them the information which as strangers they would naturally require.

"Thank you," said the Baron, who, thinking him a very polite gentleman, made him a bow. "We accept your services."

"Come then, Mynheers, come then," said the guide; "with me as your conductor, you will see more of the city in a few hours than you would by yourselves in as many days. You will understand that Amsterdam is the largest town in Holland," he commenced. "It is built in the shape of a crescent, or horse-shoe, and is situated at the influx of the Amstel into the Y; the latter, though it is called a river, is in reality an arm of the Zuyder Zee, and forms our harbour; hence the name of 'Amsterdam—the dam of the Amstel, or Amster. Now I will lead you to the docks, close to which we now are—they are capable of accommodating a thousand vessels; the locks, you will observe, are of enormous strength, which it is necessary they should be, so as to resist the inroads of the sea. We take great precautions to keep it out, and

with good reason, for our streets are much below
its level, and were it to break in they would be
completely flooded. Our city is nine miles in
circumference, while canals of various sizes intersect
it in every direction, and divide it into ninety
islands, which are connected by means of nearly
three hundred bridges. A broad moat, or canal,
also runs almost completely round it, a portion of
which is flanked with avenues of elms, which have
a handsome and picturesque appearance. Our houses
are constructed on foundations of piles, and as some
of these give way, either destroyed by worms or
becoming rotten by age, the houses are apt to lean
about in various directions, which artists say look
very picturesque, but are not so pleasant to the
inhabitants, who, however, live on in them, hoping
that, as they have been in that condition for some
years, they will not tumble down just yet. Now
and then they do come down, but people get
accustomed to that sort of thing. Many years ago
our great corn magazine sank into the mud, the
piles on which it stood being unable to support the

weight of three thousand five hundred tons of grain,
which were stored in the building at that time.
You will observe the style of the houses, many of
them built of Dutch brickwork, which foreigners
justly admire.   Our canals are not quite as deep
as they should be, although we have dredging
machines constantly engaged in removing the mud,
which is thus apt to be stirred about in an unpleasant manner as every barge comes up, and
strangers declare that an excessively offensive odour
rises from them, especially on hot days; but we
who live here are not inconvenienced, in fact we
rather doubt the statement; there may be a smell,
but it surely cannot be an unpleasant one."

"As to that," answered the Count, holding his
pocket-handkerchief to his nose, "it must depend
upon what people consider unpleasant; for my part,
I prefer the scent of orange blossoms or eau de
Cologne to it."

The guide, who seemed anxious to fulfil his
promise of enabling them to see the city in a
brief period of time, trotted them along the quays

at a rapid rate, pointing out to them the great dyke which prevents the Zuyder Zee from washing into the town; then he conducted them up one street and down another, over bridges and along banks of canals innumerable, till they had not the slightest idea of where they were going or what they were seeing. He poured out his information also at so rapid a rate that the Count could with difficulty make the shortest notes. Museums and picture galleries of various sorts were pointed out to them.

"You will be able to see those by and by," observed the guide; "at present my object is to exhibit to you the outside of the city."

The whole day was expended in viewing the city, and even then a large portion remained to be seen, which they flattered themselves they should do on another occasion. They then, pretty well tired, returned to their hotel.

"Now, Count, in what direction shall we next bend our steps?" asked the Baron. "If we were at sea the wind might settle that point, but on shore the matter is more complicated."

"Come with me, Mynheers, to Zaandam," said a gentleman, who was seated opposite to them at table and heard the Baron's question.

"I suppose there's something to be seen there?" the Baron asked.

"Certainly there is something to be seen," said the gentleman. "There's the house of Peter the Great, who lived there while he was working as a shipwright, and there are windmills."

"There are a good many windmills in other parts of Holland," observed the Count.

"But the windmills of Zaandam beat them all hollow," answered the gentleman. "There are no fewer than four hundred in and about Zaandam, employed in all sorts of labour: some grind corn, some saw timber, others crush rape-seed, while others again drain the land, or reduce stones to powder, or chop tobacco into snuff, or grind colours for the painter. Those of Zaandam are of all shapes and descriptions, and many of them are of an immense size—the largest in the world."

"We will go to Zaandam," said the Count; and

the next morning he and the Baron accompanied
their new friend, whom they took care to ascertain
was not a professional guide, down to the quay,
whence a steamboat
was about to start
to their intended
destination.

In little more
than an hour,
having crossed the
waters of the Y,

they landed at Zaandam. They were not dis-
appointed with respect to the windmills, which,
as there was a fair breeze, seemed to be all
very busy, the sails whirling round and round
and doing their duty with all earnestness, as duty
ought to be done. When the wind slackened
it was not their fault if they did not go as fast.
They could distinguish the flour mills, which
generally had a balcony running round half-way
up; but the draining mills were smaller, and had
no balcony. Zaandam, however, did not look like
a town, it more resembled a straggling village; the
houses—small, painted a bright green, with red
roofs—peeping out on the banks of the river amid
the trees in all directions.

Suddenly the Count began whirling his arms about
in a way which made the Baron fancy he had gone
mad.

" What is the matter ?" he exclaimed.

" I cannot help it," answered the Count, still
looking up at the windmills. " How they go round
and round and round in all directions; it is 'enough

L

to turn one into a windmill. I feel inclined already to become one."

" Don't, don't !" cried the Baron, seizing his friend's arms and holding them down. " Don't look at those whirlabout sails, but come let us go and see the house of Peter the Great, which was the chief object of our visit to this place."

" Peter the Great, ah, I have heard of him; how long did he live here ? " asked the Count.

" Not very long," said their friend. " Zaandam was in those days a great ship-building place, and he came here to instruct himself in the art; but the people found out who he was, and shocked his modesty by staring him out of countenance, so he went away to Amsterdam, where among the crowd he was less likely to be discovered."

Proceeding along a canal bordered by a few dilapidated houses, they arrived before a zinc building, which has been erected to cover the hut in which Peter the Great lived. An ancient individual, who had charge of it, admitted them within the outside covering.

"Peter of Russia was a great man, there's no doubt about that," observed the Baron. "But from the appearance of this edifice he must have been contented with a very inferior style of accommodation; for there appear to be but two

PETER THE GREAT'S HOUSE.

small rooms, and every plank of the walls is out of the perpendicular, and every beam far off the horizontal, while the floors resemble the surface of · a troubled sea."

The hut was constructed of wood, old planks nailed roughly together, some running in one direction, some in another. As the travellers entered they rolled about as if they had suddenly become giddy. The furniture too was limited; it consisted of a couple of curiously shaped old chairs, a table and a bedstead of antique form and simple construction. The walls were adorned with portraits of Peter the Great and his wife, who certainly, judging by her picture, was no beauty.

" I observe that a number of persons of celebrity have carved their names on the walls; I think we ought to do the same, to let it be known to all the world, who come after us, that we have been here," said the Baron, taking out his pen-knife. " Here are some names, great persons undoubtedly, and, as far as I can judge, English; let me see, one is Jones, the other is Smith, and a third Brown—we will add ours."

" Have the kindness to put mine, then," said the Count. " I should wish to appear in such excellent company, but carving on wood is not one of my talents."

The Baron accordingly with the tip of his pen-knife wrote, or rather carved, "Count Funnibos and Baron Stilkin," putting the date of their visit. Well satisfied with his performance, he took another glance round the room, about which the Count had been staggering, looking at the various corners and crevices, as if he expected to find the Great Peter in one of them, sawing or planing, or perhaps supping off a bowl of porridge. The ancient keeper informed them that the building was erected by a former Queen of Holland — a Princess of Russia—to prevent this relic of her ancestor being swept off the face of the earth. On one of the walls was a marble tablet, placed there by the Emperor Alexander to commemorate a visit he paid to the hut, which showed to the Count and Baron that another great person had been there before them.

CHAPTER IX.

N returning to the town of windmills, they encountered the gentleman who had advised them to pay a visit to the place.

"I am going on to Alkmaar," he observed, "and should be rejoiced to have your company; it is a place well worth seeing, and you will have further experience of Dutch scenery on the way."

"We will go, by all means," said the Count, who, as it saved him the trouble of thinking, was glad to receive suggestions regarding their route. They accordingly went on board the steamer, which was already pretty well filled with country people, butter-sellers, pedlers, gardeners, and others, very clean and respectable and picturesque in their

costume. There was a vast amount of shouting
and holloaing and talking as the boat passed
through a narrow lock, which conducted them into
the direct line of canal navigation to the place
they purposed visiting. As they glided on, they
observed the banks on either side lined with windmills; here and there were small houses painted
green with red roofs—indeed, red roofs were seen
everywhere, like British soldiers skirmishing, as
the colour was toned down and mellowed by time
and weather. On and on they went, sometimes
looking down from the canal to the country below
them, for the water was on a higher level than
the land.

"It would be an awkward business if a breach
were to be made in the banks, and the water
were to run out over the country," observed the
Count.

"We take precautions against that, by making
the banks broad and strong, as you will observe,"
remarked their friend. "But such an event has
occurred more than once, sometimes by accident,

and at others purposely, to prevent the approach of an enemy, when in a few hours a whole district has been laid under water."

"When that occurs, the fields and the orchards and the cottages of the inhabitants must be destroyed," observed the Count.

"Undoubtedly," answered his companion. "But we Dutchmen are patriotic, and willingly sacrifice our own interests for the good of the country; besides which the chief sufferers have seldom been consulted—our leaders have decided that it was necessary, and it has been done. In this way Alkmaar was defended against the Spaniards, and Leyden was relieved by a fleet of the 'Beggars of the Sea,' which, sailing across the submerged land, brought provisions and reinforcements to the starving garrison."

League after league was passed over by this watery way; trees there were, but they were scarcely of sufficient height to break the uniform appearance of the level country.

"My dear Baron," said the Count, taking his

friend by the button-hole, "I have at length settled a point in my mind which has long puzzled me; I have heard that philosophers differ as to whether the earth is round or flat, and now you will agree with me that we have proof positive that it is flat. Look round on every side —the country is as level as a billiard table, the water in the canals does not run one way more than another, there's not a single elevation between us and the distant horizon. Yes, I am convinced of the fact: one does learn something by travelling."

The Baron, who was seldom in an argumentative mood, smiled blandly, and replied, "Yes, my dear Count, you are probably right as far as Holland is concerned. When we reach other parts of the world we may be compelled, against our better judgment, to change our opinion, but time enough for that when we get there; let us at present side with those who hold to the opinion that the world is flat, but not with those who pronounce it stale and unprofitable, for Holland is certainly not unprofitable, or the people would not look so wealthy, fat, and comfortable."

After the canal had made several turnings, the tall steeples of Alkmaar, quaint and ancient, appeared in sight, but it was some time before the steamer reached the quay of that picturesque town.

Leaving the steamboat, the Count and the Baron at once going to an hotel, ordered dinner to be prepared, having invited their new friend to join them.

"Though Alkmaar is a place of no great importance at present," observed their friend, "it can boast of three things—its heroic defence against the Spaniards, of which I will give you an account by-and-by as we walk round the ramparts; of its cleanliness, of which you have ocular proof; and of the vast amount of excellent cheese which it exports; indeed, it is said to do more business in cheese than any other town in the world. There are also two or three quaint and curious buildings which are worthy of a visit."

"We will visit them in their turn," observed the Baron.

As he descended the steps of the hotel he evidently created some sensation among the market people, fishwives, the butter-sellers, and others who thronged the streets. Perceiving this, he stopped short and looked about him with a benignant air. "Perhaps, if I were to take up my residence here, I might be elected Burgomaster," he thought to himself, "though at home it might be beneath my

rank to enter into commerce. I should have no objection to deal in cheese, they look so clean, and taste so nice, and have so fragrant an odour. A million cheeses exported by Baron Stilkin and Co. would sound well, and even though I were to make a profit of only a styver per cheese, would come to a good sum annually—I will see to it." His cogitations were interrupted by the appearance of the Count and their friend, who now invited him to accompany them round the town. Their friend was an enthusiastic patriot, and having shown them Alkmaar, and described its heroic defence against the Spaniards, advised them as to the course they should afterwards pursue. They accordingly set off and visited Haarlem and Leyden, the Hague—the royal capital—and Rotterdam, the great commercial city rivalling Amsterdam, Gouda, and Utrecht, which possesses a cathedral and a fine old tower rising to the height of three hundred and twenty feet above the ground.

"And now I propose that, as we have seen all these towns, we go forth and enjoy something of the country, before we leave Holland," said the Count.

"Agreed," answered the Baron, and so it was settled.

CHAPTER X.

ONCE more the Count and the Baron were in the country. As yet they had made but little progress in their journey round the world, but they were not disheartened.

"We shall do it in time," remarked the Count. "And it strikes me that if we were to put on my seven-league boots we should go much faster."

"But, my dear Count, have you seen them lately?" asked the Baron. "A dreadful idea has occurred to me. I am afraid that I left one of them on board of the *Golden Hog*, and if she has gone to the bottom your seven-league boot has gone also, and with only one it is very clear that we shall not go ahead with the desirable rapidity."

"Then I suspect we must do without them,"

said the Count, who always took matters easily. "We must depend upon our own legs and such means of conveyance as present themselves. With the help of the railways, steamboats, trackboats, and horse carriages, we may still manage to get along. By-the-by, could we not manage to engage a balloon? We might get over the country at greater speed than even with my seven-league boots."

"We should not see much of it in that way, I suspect," observed the Baron.

"Oh, yes! A fine bird's-eye view, such as an eagle enjoys," exclaimed the Count.

"I decidedly object to aërial travelling," said the Baron. "It does not suit my figure, and I always feel giddy if I look down from a height. Sailing on the treacherous ocean is bad enough, and even railways are not altogether satisfactory. Give me the firm ground, a nice easy chaise on four wheels, steady horses, and an experienced coachman, and I can enjoy travelling. But here we are at Night-erecht, a pleasant, rural-looking place. It boasts of an inn, though not a large one, but we can enjoy the primitive simplicity of the inhabitants."

On reaching the inn, having announced themselves, they were received by the landlady with all the courtesy and respect due to persons of their exalted rank.

"We must ask you, good Vrouw, to direct us to any objects worthy of inspection in this neighbourhood, that we may visit them while you are preparing dinner," said the Baron.

"Objects worthy of inspection," said the Vrouw; "there are the houses, and the fields, and the canals, we have two — one passing close to the village, the other a little way in the rear—and five windmills, all in sight without the trouble of going in search of them. We expect that there will be something too which will take place to interest your lordships this afternoon. A stranger arrived this morning with a cart containing a large cask, the contents of which he proposes to exhibit to all those who will pay him a guilder each; the guilders are to remain with him, the contents of the cask are to be divided among the spectators. You will, of course, Mynheers, remain to witness the spectacle, and to enjoy the benefits which may be derived from the contents of the cask. Some say it is full of one thing, some of another, but no one knows what. Notices have been sent round in all directions, and we expect to have a numerous gathering, which will, at all events, prove profitable to my establishment."

The Count and the Baron, not being hurried, agreed to remain. As soon as dinner was over they observed a number of persons collecting under the trees in front of the inn, which stood, as the landlady assured them, on the top of a mountain, though the descent to the canal was scarcely more than twenty feet, comparing it with the level region around. In a short time a burly individual appeared, and, with the aid of two or three others, placed a huge cask on a central spot under the trees with the head facing down the hill. He then forthwith took his seat astride on the top of it.

"Now, noble Mynheers and lovely Vrouws, you

have come to see something very wonderful; but before I exhibit the mystery I must request you to hand me in the guilders, for unless I obtain a sufficient number the cask remains closed."

The people were flocking in from all parts, for at that time of the evening they had nothing in particular to do. The Count and the Baron drew near. The burly personage astride of the cask continued his address, while two or three attendants who had come with him went round to collect the coin.

" You will understand, brave Hollanders, that any one who is disposed to give two guilders or three guilders is welcome to do so, and will, I hope, reap a proportionate reward," he cried out at the top of his voice.

The Count, who had become much interested, wondering what was coming out of the cask, proposed putting in five guilders.

" As you like," observed the Baron, " but it is wise, as a rule, to know what you are going to get for your money, and I suggest that we promise

the individual on the cask an ample reward should
we be satisfied.   It would be as well not to pay
more than anybody else."

"But then we can scarcely claim the privilege of
standing in the front rank," observed the Count.
"Come, he shall have two guilders."

"As you like, it will save me the necessity of
putting my hand in my purse," said the Baron.

The attendants having collected all the money
they were likely to get, the individual on the cask,
in a sonorous voice, announced his intention of
exhibiting its contents. For some time past there
had been strange noises proceeding from it, the
cause of which no one could understand.

"Are you prepared to see what you shall see?"
cried the stout individual, riding astride on the
cask. "Make ready, then. One, two, three;" and
by some contrivance or other, he suddenly caused
the head of the cask to fall out to the ground.
when a chorus of mews and feline shrieks and
cries as if long pent up burst forth, followed by
an avalanche of cats with labels fixed to their

tails; who, gazing for a moment at the assemblage, dashed frantically forward, some in one direction, some in another, blinded by the light suddenly let in on their eyes: one made a rush at the Baron, and had almost seized his chin, while her claws stuck into his shirt-front before he could knock her off; another made a dash at the Count, who fled precipitately. Each cat, perhaps with the impression that she was ascending a tree, sprang first at one of the bystanders, and then at another; and then, if driven aside, dashed frantically forward down the slope, upsetting half a dozen of the spectators as they endeavoured to make their escape.

"I told you, Mynheers and lovely Vrouws, that I should astonish you," exclaimed the stout individual on the cask. "Each of you shall be welcome to the cats you can catch." A few boys and girls, who seemed to consider it great fun, made chase after the cats. The Count and the Baron, and not a few other persons, being considerably irate at the hoax that had been practised upon them, turned furiously towards the burly individual, who still kept his seat on the cask.

"How dare you sit there laughing at us!" exclaimed one.

"You impudent fellow! you deserve to be ducked in the canal," cried another.

"You will only receive your due if we kick you out of the village," cried a third.

"A very proper way to treat him," exclaimed a fourth.

"Then let us begin!" exclaimed a fifth.

The stout individual, finding the tide of public favour had decidedly turned against him, leaped off his cask, and fought his way through the angry crowd, who had, fortunately for him, been somewhat dispersed by the cats. Some tried to catch him, others tried to trip him up; but he was a stout fellow, and was not to be easily caught. Dodging in and out among them, till seeing a narrow lane which no one at the moment was guarding, he dashed down it, hoping to make his escape from the village; but instead of leading him to the outside, as he had hoped, it conducted him to the very centre. On he ran, followed by the whole crowd, the Count and Baron joining in the hue and cry. The village resounded with shouts of "Stop thief! stop thief!" but these only made the burly individual run the faster. A few of the

inhabitants had made a
short cut, hoping to meet
him in front; but they
only arrived in time to
catch him by the skirts
of his coat, which gave way as he sprang by
them; several others made a grab at him, some
at the collar, some on one side, some on the

other, till the coat was reduced to shreds, when slipping his arms out of it he again sprang forward. The Count and the Baron, who had been rushing on with the crowd, were by some means or other separated. The Count having lost sight of the chase, thinking after all that it was no business of his, returned to his inn. It would have been well for the Baron if he had done the same; but as he was running on at a more rapid rate than he was wont to move, he tripped and fell; the rest of those engaged in the pursuit, in their eagerness scarcely perceiving what had happened, passed him by, leaving him to regain his legs as best he could. As soon as he had got up, he went on again at less speed, and in a more cautious manner.

"I should like to see that fellow castigated," he said to himself. "Never was served a more abominable trick. Where can he have gone? If I don't make haste I shall not see what happens." He accordingly ran on again; now he turned up one narrow lane, now down another, till he had completely lost himself. "It cannot be a large place, however," he thought, "and I shall easily find my way back to the inn. Ah! I think I hear the shouts of the people."

He began to run on; presently he distinguished cries of, "There he is, there he is! That must be he, just his size! We'll catch him now!"

"I hope they will," thought the Baron, and on he went; but as he happened to turn and glance over his shoulder, to his surprise, he saw that the people were following him. "We shall have him now! we shall have him now!" he heard the mob shouting. "That must be he! He is up to all sorts of tricks. Take care he does not escape us. Stop thief! stop thief!"

The Baron not liking the sounds, and fearing that there might be some mistake, thought it best to keep ahead of the mob, and bolted down the first opening he discovered. To his great satisfaction, at the further end, he saw not only the inn, but the Count standing at the door of it. The mob were close behind him, now excited more than ever by their running, uttering all sorts of threats, and making unpleasant gestures with their fists, sticks, and staves.

The Count looked astonished, scarcely comprehending what was happening. Never had the Baron run so fast, puffing and blowing as he went, and expecting every moment to drop from fatigue. Several persons were collected about the door of the inn, who seemed to be amused at watching him as he ran. At that moment two baker's boys, carrying between them a large basketful of pies and cakes and loaves, and some paper bags of flour, happened to be passing the inn door. The Baron, in his hurry not seeing them, ran against the basket, when over he went with his legs in the air, his arms and shoulders and the larger part of his body into the very middle of the pies and cakes and bags of flour. The boys with looks of alarm held on firmly to the handles, without making any attempt to assist him, while he, overcome by his unusual exertions, was utterly unable to help himself. The Count, for the moment, was too much

astonished   to   do
anything, but stood
with   arms   uplifted
exclaiming, "My dear Baron, what has happened?
Do get out of that;" while other persons who
stood by only cruelly grinned at his misfortune.

At length the Count, recovering his presence of mind, descended the steps to the assistance of the hapless Baron, who certainly was more frightened than hurt, though covered from head to foot with flour and dough and the contents of the meat pies and fruit tarts, producing an extraordinary and ludicrous effect.

The mob, who had by this time come up, shouted, "We have him at last. Now where shall we carry him to? What shall we do with him? He has given us a pretty long chase, and deserves to be well ducked, or tarred and feathered!"

"My dear people," exclaimed the Count, "you have made a mistake; this is my friend, Baron Stilkin, who joined you in the chase of that roguish fellow who let the cats out of the cask, and whom I am afraid you let go as well as the cats."

The mob still insisted that the Baron was the man of whom they were in chase, and it required all the Count's eloquence to persuade them to the contrary; but his pitiable plight rather amused them than excited their compassion. Some of them had even the cruelty to beg him to start again, and give them another chase. At length the kind-hearted landlady of the inn, coming out, begged him to enter, undertaking to wash his waistcoat and shirt front, and to put him to rights.

"Thanks, my good Vrouw, thanks; and if you will prepare some supper for me, I shall be doubly grateful, for I am terribly hungry after my long run," answered the Baron.

"First let me get off the paste and flour, jam and grease," said the Vrouw, bringing a brush and a towel and water; and she rubbed and scrubbed for some minutes with such good effect that the Baron's garments were restored to their primitive lustre.

"And now my outward appearance has been polished up, pray look after the interests of my inner man," said the Baron, placing his hands to his heart. "I shall ever bear in mind the polite attention with which you have treated me, though it will take some time to forget the want of dis-cernment your townsmen have exhibited in mistaking me for that abominable cat-man. What could have induced him to play such a trick?"

The landlady admitted that she had met no one who could solve the mystery.

"Nor have I," said the Count. "I have been making inquiries in all directions, but not a person has been able to give me the wished-for information."

While the Vrouw went off to prepare supper for the Count and Baron, they seated themselves at a table in the neat little guest room to wait for it. Directly afterwards in came one of the bakers' boys, demanding payment for the pies and tarts, the puddings and flour, injured and scattered by the Baron.

"Pay you for getting in my way and causing me to fall over your abominable basket, to the great injury of my waistcoat and shirt front, breeches and coat; not to speak of the undignified position I was compelled to assume amid the jeers and laughter of the surrounding populace!" exclaimed the Baron, eyeing the small baker's boy.

"I am told by my master to demand payment, and payment he says he must have," answered the small baker's boy.

"Our wisest course will be to pay the demand made on us, and I would advise you in future not to tumble into a baker's basket if you can help it," said the Count.

The Count, who was always open-handed, paid the demand made on the Baron, to the infinite satisfaction of the small baker's boy. The Baron's spirits revived after he had done justice to the supper prepared by the kind-hearted Vrouw.

"In what direction shall we next bend our steps?" asked the Count.

"I have a fancy to visit the province of Guelderland, the region of roses; and afterwards Friesland, celebrated throughout Holland for the beauty of its fair dames and its ancient and interesting cities," answered the Baron.

"How shall we travel?" asked the Count.

"I have been giving the matter my earnest consideration," answered the Baron, "and I have arrived at the conclusion that the easiest, the pleasantest, if not the most expeditious, mode of travelling will be by *Trek-Schuit*, or canal boat, where we can sit at our ease or sleep and eat while we are dragged smoothly on over the placid water."

" Certainly, the idea is an excellent one," said the Count, who was always ready to do what the Baron proposed.

Accordingly the next morning, as the *Trek-Schuit* was passing the village, they took their seats on board, and proceeded on their journey.

CHAPTER XI.

THE *Trek-Schuit* is a long canal-boat, divided into two compartments, forming a first and second class, and is drawn by a trotting horse along the towing-path. It contains seats well cushioned for sleeping, a table for meals, and every other convenience for ease-loving people who are not in a hurry. A pleasanter mode of conveyance cannot be conceived; there is no shaking or vibration; in rainy weather the cabin is warm and comfortable, and in fine weather the passenger can sit on deck and watch the fast receding landscape. Such was the character of the boat in which the Count and Baron were now travelling. The scenery need not be minutely described; but it

N

presented a pleasing level on every side, and the canal being in many places raised above the surrounding country, they could look down from their seat on the deck of the boat on the corn-fields and broad green meadows, scattered over with farmhouses and cottages, and occasionally with a few trees. Windmills of course very often made their appearance, and cows, generally black and white, but mixed sometimes with a few red ones, were to be seen on every hand. The scenery, though unvaried, was not wearisome, especially when the sun shone brightly; and the fields looked fresh and green, and the water sparkled, and everywhere marks of man's industry were to be seen. Sometimes locks had to be passed, and the boat either ascended or descended a few feet, but it was not often she left the usual level. The particulars of the journey need not be detailed, as no adventures of especial interest were met with. Leaving the *Trek-Schuit* they continued their journey on land, having engaged a vehicle of antique form, the box handsomely sculptured, highly coloured and gilt,

and the harness well burnished. It was drawn by
a fine black horse ornamented with red bows.
They stepped in, and away they dashed at a rapid
rate along the well-kept road. At length, early
one afternoon, they alighted at a small inn, where
they resolved to remain for a day or two, that
they might become better acquainted with the
country and its inhabitants than they could be
either by gliding through it on board a *Trek-
Schuit*, or galloping along the road in a vehicle.

"Now," said the Baron, after he and the Count
had satisfied the cravings of the inner man, "let
us go forth in search of adventures." They walked
along arm-in-arm, as was their wont, looking about
them.

"Ah, what do I see!" exclaimed the Count. "A
pretty villa, embowered by trees! a rarity in these
regions. I wonder whether the inhabitants are as
attractive as their residence: so lovely a spot may
be the abode of the most graceful of sylphs. Even
at this distance we can see what pretty creepers
adorn its trellised porch; how green the lawn, how

bright are the flowers;
and see, yonder, how
the blue river dotted
by white sails sparkles
in the sunlight!"

"Ah, very beautiful, but I should not be surprised
to find it inhabited by some stout double-fisted
Vrouw or surly old bachelor," said the Baron.

The Count and the Baron walked on till they reached the garden, which was separated from the road by a light paling. On more level ground it would have been by a moat or ditch.

"Ah!" exclaimed the Count. "My dear Baron, there are two young ladies seated among the roses, charming and graceful, instead of the old Vrouw you predicted we should find; and there is a little girl with her doll on the grass, and in the porch I see an elderly lady with a young boy. What a beautiful family picture!"

"Ah! but do you not observe that elderly gentleman with spectacles, smoking his pipe," said the Baron, as they advanced a few steps, and the individual spoken of came into sight. "He regards us with no friendly gaze through those spectacles of his, as if he already looked on us with suspicion."

"We will hope that his thoughts are of a more amiable character," said the Count. "At all events, let us approach, and show him that we are worthy of any attentions he may be disposed to bestow on us."

"Come along, then; bashfulness is not among the list of my vices," said the Baron. And together they advanced to the palings, when, simultaneously taking off their hats, they each made a profound bow to the two ladies, when the old gentleman, with spectacles on his nose and pipe in his hand, standing near the flower basket, turned round his head and regarded them with an inquiring glance.

"This is my friend, Count Funnibos," said the Baron; whereon the Count, making another bow towards the old gentleman with the spectacles, said, "And this is my friend and travelling companion, Baron Stilkin," on which the Baron made a bow towards the old gentleman in spectacles and another towards the young ladies seated among the roses, who gracefully bent their heads in recognition of the compliment. The old gentleman, not to be outdone in civility, advancing a few paces, made two polite bows in return.

"Come, we have produced some impression," whispered the Baron to the Count. "We must not let the grass grow under our feet. I will speak

to them. Most excellent and esteemed Mynheer,"
he said, "Count Funnibos and I are travellers
round the world, imbued with a desire to see everything interesting, beautiful, wonderful, and strange
on our way, and especially the habits and customs
of the inhabitants of the countries we visit. We
shall therefore esteem it a favour if you will allow
us to make your acquaintance, and that of your
charming family. Those young ladies are, I presume, your daughters, and your excellent Vrouw,
seated under the porch, is, I conclude, affording
instruction to one of the younger members of your
family."

"You are perfectly right, Mynheers. As you
have announced you names, I am bound to inform
you that mine is Hartog Van Arent, those three
ladies are my daughters, and the elder lady is my
Vrouw, to whom I shall have the happiness of
introducing you if you will come through the gate
you will find a little further on near the house."

Again the Count and Baron bowed, and expressed
the honour they should feel at being introduced to

the Vrouw Van Arent and her charming daughters.
The young ladies, on hearing this, smiled sweetly,
and rising from their seats approached the house to
be in readiness to be introduced to the strangers.
The Vrouw welcomed them cordially, as Dutch
ladies are accustomed to receive guests, and the
young ladies were not behind their mother in that
respect, while the little girl ran up with her doll,
which she held up to be admired, thinking more
of it than herself. In a few minutes the Count
and the Baron made themselves perfectly at home,
as if they had known the family all their lives.
Mynheer Van Arent invited them to enter the
house, and after partaking of an early supper, they
spent a pleasant evening. The young ladies played
the piano and sang, if not artistically, with sweet
voices, so that the Count and the Baron professed
themselves completely captivated. They were considering it time to take their departure, when
another guest was announced, and a gentleman
entered who was received by Mynheer Van Arent
and his Vrouw in as cordial a manner as they

had been. He was introduced to the Count and the Baron as Mynheer Bunckum. He made them a somewhat stiff bow, which they returned with their usual politeness. He evidently was taking great pains to make himself agreeable to the young ladies, who seemed, however, not over-inclined to encourage his attentions.

At last, pulling out his watch, he observed that it was getting late, looking at the Count and the Baron at the same time as a hint to them to take their departure; but they waited till he had made his bow and retired, then, after some more agreeable conversation, they also bowed themselves out of the house.

" Truly," observed the Count, " this has been the pleasantest evening we have spent since we started on our travels."

" So pleasant that I presume you will wish to spend some more of the same character," remarked the Baron.

" Indeed I do," said the Count. " For, to confess the truth, I have lost my heart."

"Have you, indeed!" exclaimed the Baron. "To which of the fair ladies, may I ask?"

"That remains as yet a secret unknown to myself," said the Count. "They are both so charming."

"Pray, as soon as you can discover the secret, do not conceal it from me," said the Baron. "I have particular reasons for asking."

All this time they were not aware that they were closely followed by some one, who must have heard every word they said. Suddenly the sound of a footfall reached their ears, and turning they saw a figure, who, finding that he was discovered, rapidly retreated.

"Stop!" cried the Count, "whoever you are; we wish to have a few words with you."

"Stop, I say!" repeated the Baron. But their shouts were unheeded, and neither of them felt inclined to give chase.

"Who can that be?" asked the Count.

"That is the question," answered the Baron. "What do you say to Mynheer Bunckum? He cast

a jealous eye at us, as if he considered we were rivals."

"Then he should have come up and spoken to us like a man," said the Count. "We must be on our guard, at all events, for he evidently has no friendly feeling towards us."

The Count and the Baron met with no further adventures till they reached the inn.

CHAPTER XII.

THE next morning the Count and the Baron rose from their downy slumbers and took breakfast, to which the Baron paid due attention, as he did, in truth, to all his meals.

"Now, my dear Baron, what do you say—shall we continue our journey, or again pay our respects to the estimable family of Van Arent?" asked the Count.

"At this hour, I fear, from what I know of the habits of the people, that our visit would not be welcome," said the Baron. "The young ladies are probably engaged in milking the cows, or making butter, or superintending the manufacture of cheese. We should catch them in their working-dresses, and be considered intruders."

"Then the best thing we can do is to sally forth and see the country," said the Count. "But yet I should not like to leave this part of it without again having the happiness of basking in the smiles of those charming young ladies, Vrouw Margaret and Vrouw Isabella."

"I think you may be content with basking in the smiles of one of the two," remarked the Baron. "I flatter myself that the smiles of the other are directed towards me."

"We won't quarrel on the matter," said the Count, who greatly disliked to dispute. "I was going to tell you that I have an idea."

"Have you, indeed!" exclaimed the Baron. "It is not often you indulge in anything of the sort. Pray let me know what it is."

"My idea is this," said the Count. "You know that I am an exquisite player on the violin, though I did not bring one with me; for I might have been mistaken, had I done so, for an itinerant musician. The idea that has occurred to me is that I will purchase one, so that I may be able to accompany the fair Vrouws when they play the piano. They are sure to be delighted, and I shall be raised still higher in their good graces."

"You are only thinking of yourself," muttered the Baron. "But suppose," he added aloud, "no violin is to be found in this rural district, how can you obtain one?"

"I propose that we proceed to the nearest town, where such instruments are sure to be on sale; and we can return by the evening, when we are more likely to be admitted into Mynheer Van Arent's family circle," said the Count. "You, Baron, surely play on some instrument, and you might obtain it at the same time."

"The only instruments I play are the Jew's harp and the kettle-drum, and I am afraid that neither are very well suited to entertain ladies in their drawing-room," said the Baron.

"Not exactly. The latter would be rather too cumbersome to carry about," said the Count. "However, let us set forth, or we shall not have time to return before the evening." Fortunately they found a *Trek-Schuit* just starting for the far-famed town of Sneek.

Occasionally the boat passed between some of the small towns and villages they had seen afar off, composed of neat houses with yellow and blue blinds The housewives, in golden casques, the usual head-dress, standing at the doors often exhibited a bright copper jug glistening in the sun. The travellers frequently passed numerous boats, the men on board of which saluted them politely. They appeared good-natured, happy fellows, with ruddy countenances, light hair, and rings hanging to their ears. They were mostly dressed in red shirts, blue and white knickerbockers fastened at the knee, and thick brown woollen stockings. The boat, as she glided on, was generally accompanied by sea-gulls, storks with long legs and outstretched necks, flights of lapwings, and other species of the feathered tribe, uttering their plaintive cries, and ever and anon as they skimmed the waves diving below the water to bring some hapless fish in their long slender beaks.

"Here we are," cried the Count, as they glided

into the picturesque little town of Sneek, with its houses of white woodwork and painted window-frames, its winding streets and high-arched bridges, its trees and shady walks along the canals, its gaily-painted canal-boats, and its picturesque water-gate. The town itself was soon inspected, while the Count and the Baron on their way made inquiries for the instrument the former was anxious to purchase. They were almost giving up the search in despair, when they heard of a manufacturer who was said to have produced violins which, in the hands of an artist, were capable of giving forth such touching sounds that many who heard them were moved to tears.

"That is just the description of instrument I require," exclaimed the Count.

He and the Baron hastened on to the shop of the manufacturer. It was an ancient building, the front of which looked as if, before long, it would become acquainted with the roadway. There were not only violins, but other musical instruments and curiosities of all sorts.

"Before I part with the violin I must hear you play," said the vendor; "I never allow my instruments to go into unskilled hands."

The Count eagerly took the violin, and played a few notes. The Baron produced his pocket-handkerchief, and placed it to his eyes.

"Touching, very touching!" he exclaimed.

"You will do," said the vendor.

The Count, well pleased with his purchase, asked the Baron if he could find any instrument to suit him.

The Baron shook his head, mournfully. "I must depend on my voice; and, provided I do not catch a cold, that will, I hope, produce as much effect as your fiddle."

"We shall see," said the Count.

Leaving the shop, they hastened back to the *Trek-Schuit*, which was about to return the way they had come. The journey occupied so long a time that the shades of evening were already stealing over the landscape when they reached their inn. Though the Count was eager at once to set out

o

for the house of Mynheer Van Arent, the Baron declared that, without his supper, he could not sing at all. By the time that was finished it was dark.

"Now," said the Count, "let us go; even for you, Baron, I cannot wait longer."

The Count, of course, carried his violin.

"As it is too late to present ourselves, we will remain outside among the trees. You shall play an air, and I will sing a song, and we will then go in and ascertain the effect," said the Baron.

They soon got to a part of the shrubbery where they could effectually conceal themselves. Overhead they observed a tall tree—one of the branches of which extended to the walls of the house.

"Now," whispered the Baron, "shall I sing, or will you commence an air on your violin?"

"I will begin," said the Count, who was on the point of drawing the bow across the strings, when the Baron grasped his arm.

"Hark!" he said; "look up there."

What was their astonishment to observe a figure climbing the ancient tree they had remarked close above them. They, at all events, had not been discovered. Higher and higher the person climbed, till he gained a bough extending towards the house. Along it he made his way. When near the end, he stopped and threw several pieces of a branch he broke off against the shutter of a window, which was at no great distance from where he stood.

The Count, thus interrupted in his intended serenade, with jealous eyes watched the proceedings of the stranger, fully expecting that either Vrouw Margaret or Vrouw Isabelle would appear at the window. At length it opened, when, instead, the more portly form of Vrouw Van Arent herself came into view. She gazed with open eyes at the stranger standing up on the bough of the tree.

"Who are you, who thus, in so unseemly a way, ventures to disturb the quiet of our abode?" she asked, in somewhat angry tones.

"Hist, hist, Vrouw Van Arent! I am Ten Dick Bunckum. Not wishing to appear in the presence of your fair daughters, I have taken this

method of warning you of a danger which threatens your family. Yesterday evening two persons were received in your house, who pretend to be a Count and a Baron. I have strong evidence, if not proof positive, that they are strolling musicians, who are travelling about the country to prey on the unwary. My great desire is to put you on your guard against them."

"I am much obliged to you for your good intentions, Mynheer Bunckum, but would rather you had taken some other method of warning me, instead of throwing sticks at this window."

"I could not tell whether those pretended Count and Baron were already in your house; and, as my object was to avoid meeting them, I climbed into this tree that I might wait till I saw you approach the window."

"The Count and Baron have not come to the house this evening, and I would advise you, Mynheer Bunckum, to descend from your perilous position, and allow my husband and me to arrange our family affairs as we think right and best; and I must again beg you to get off that tree, and take care, as you do so, that you do not fall down and break your neck."

"I obey you, Vrouw Van Arent," answered Mynheer Bunckum, cautiously retracing his steps along the branch, while the lady of the mansion shut the window, and closed the shutter over it, which completely excluded the light.

The Count and the Baron meantime waited in
their place of concealment, fully believing that
Mynheer Bunckum, on reaching the ground, would
discover them. They had no wish that he should
do this, as it would show him that they were
aware of his malignant designs. They therefore
drew close under the bushes, scarcely venturing to
breathe. They could hear him, as he reached the
ground, threatening vengeance on their heads. He
passed so close to them that the Baron, by catching hold of his leg, might have tripped him up,
and punished him for his false accusations; but
they wisely allowed him to go on, as they considered that such a proceeding would not be calculated to raise them in the estimation of
Mynheer Van Arent and his family. They waited
till he had got to some distance when, coming out
of their place of concealment, they followed him
to ascertain in what direction he was going. He
was evidently too much put out to venture that
evening into the presence of the ladies.

On the way to their inn they naturally looked

about them to the right hand and to the left, as
well as occasionally behind, to be certain that
their jealous rival, as they considered Mynheer
Bunckum, was not following them. He all the time
was engaged in forming a design against their
liberties of which they had no notion. On reaching the inn, they found a note on pink paper in a
delicate female hand purporting to come from
Mynheer Van Arent, inviting them to accompany
his family to a picnic on the banks of the Meer
on the following morning.

"By all means we will go," exclaimed the Count.
"I will take my violin, and who knows what may
happen."

In the course of conversation they made inquiries
about the various people in the neighbourhood of
the landlady, whose good graces they had won.

"What sort of a person is Mynheer Bunckum?"
asked the Count.

"He owns the castle of Wykel, not far from
this. It is said that he is trying to win the hand
of one of the daughters of Mynheer Van Arent, but

whether or not he will gain her is a question. I desire to put you on your guard against him, Mynheers, for he is not a man to be trifled with."

Proceeding at an early hour the next morning to the house of Mynheer Van Arent, they found the family prepared for their excursion. The distance to the lake was not great, and on reaching the pier, running out a short distance into the shallow water, a large boat of substantial build was seen alongside. She of course was round-sterned, drawing but little water, but had tolerably sharp bows; her poop was gilded and carved, as was her stern, while every part was either varnished or brilliantly coloured. She was indeed the family yacht. Instead of white canvas her sails were of a dark red hue, though of fine material; she had a comfortably fitted-up cabin, with every luxury on board. Numberless other vessels, broad and shallow, were sailing here and there over the lake, their sails either red brick or saffron-coloured, reflected on the violet-tinted waters, which contrasted with the silvery hue of the sky, and a green ribbon of

land bordering the lake.   These flat-bottomed, bulg-
ing round vessels were employed in distributing the
produce of the neighbouring farms to all parts of
the country around.

A short sail on board the yacht took the party
to the point which had been selected for their
picnic, at which other yachts of a similar construction quickly arrived, and the viands they had
brought were then carried on shore, and spread
under the shade of the trees.   Mynheer Bunckum
before long made his appearance, looking gloomy
and morose, as he observed the strangers.   The
Count and the Baron were introduced to a number
of persons, who did their best to make themselves
agreeable.   The feast having concluded, at which
if there was not much wit there was a great deal
of laughter, the party retreated to a more shady
spot, where the Count was requested to favour
them with an air on his violin.   He gladly com-
plied, and elicited general applause, greatly to the
annoyance of Mynheer Bunckum, who, getting up,
retired to a distance, and sat himself down, fishing-

rod in hand, on a point which projected into the lake, as if such music was not worth listening to.

Meantime a boat had arrived on the beach containing three or four urchins from a neighbouring village, one of whom climbed up on a bank overlooking the spots where the party were collected, and the dinner cloth was spread. He had so placed himself that he could make a signal to his companions: two of these shortly afterwards getting out of their boat, and seeing him beckon, cautiously crept along the shore towards where the party had been enjoying their meal. There was no doubt about their object : they filled not only their capacious pockets, but some large handkerchiefs which they had brought, with everything on which they could lay their hands, especially the silver spoons and forks and other plate. Then at a sign from their companion they rapidly retreated, he quickly following, unnoticed by Mynheer Bunckum or any one else. On reaching their boat, away they pulled with their booty, and were soon out of sight. The Baron and two or three other gentlemen, whose appetites had not been fully satisfied, returned shortly after this to the table, if so it could be called, and though they observed that some of the things had been disarranged, it did not occur to them that the spot had been visited by robbers.

The Baron was the last to leave and return to the
ladies.   Not till the servants came to pack up the
plates and dishes, and knives and forks, was the
robbery discovered.   Just then Mynheer Bunckum,
who had got tired of fishing, and had returned to
the   table, on   hearing that several articles were
missing, exclaimed :

"I know who is the robber, I saw what that
Baron was about.   I shall now be able to prove
that my suspicions were correct !"

He, however, made no further remark at the
time, so that the harmony which had prevailed
during the picnic was not disturbed.   On the approach of evening the various parties separated to
their different homes.   The Count and the Baron
accompanied Mynheer Van Arent and his family to
theirs, whence after a friendly farewell they returned
to their inn.

CHAPTER XIII.

THE day following the picnic on the Meer, the Count and the Baron set out to pay a visit to the Van Arent family. As yet, however, they could not tell whether the courteous treatment they had received was simply owing to their being strangers of rank. The Count fancied that his performances on the violin, and the Baron supposed that his fascinating powers of conversation, and other attractive qualities, had something to do with it. On reaching the house they were told that the ladies had gone to take a walk at some distance.

"Perhaps we may meet them," said the Count to the Baron.

They inquired of the servant in what direction the ladies had gone. He pointed to the northward, and they set out; they walked on and on till they arrived at a wood, such as is not often found in that part of the country, and they observed an ancient tower with battlements rising up amid the trees.

" This looks like an interesting place," observed the Count, " let us explore it."

" By all means," answered the Baron. And they walked on with that air of curiosity generally exhibited by strangers when arriving at a place worth seeing.

" Fine trees and shady walks, really my castle scarcely exhibits anything finer; if I marry the fair Isabelle, it's just the sort of place I should like to possess; but we may pay it a hurried visit," said the Count.

" Then it is the Vrouw Isabelle on whom your regards are fixed?" observed the Baron.

"It was but a slip of my tongue," said the Count. " I did not intend to betray my secret."

" All right, my dear Count; to say the truth, my

heart has been captivated by the Vrouw Margaret, so that we shall not be rivals."

" That is a fortunate circumstance," observed the Count, in a somewhat supercilious tone. " However, you must remember that we, both of us, have to ascertain the feelings of the ladies; at present we are left somewhat in the dark on that subject."

" I cannot say that I think so," answered the Baron, drawing up his shirt collar. " I flatter my-self that the Vrouw Margaret regards me with peculiar distinction."

" Did I possess more vanity in this case, I might have said the same with regard to Vrouw Isabelle," said the Count.

" You do, do you ! " exclaimed a voice from among the bushes, which made the Count and the Baron start.

" Who could that have been?" exclaimed the Count.

" Where did it come from ?" cried the Baron.

" Let us try to discover the eavesdropper," said the Count.

"We had better not," whispered the Baron. "Depend upon it the person, whoever he is, is prepared for us. We had better move on, and not in future talk so loudly of our private affairs."

"Your advice is good," said the Count; "we will follow it."

And they moved on a short distance, paying much less attention than before to the beauties of the scenery. They had just reached the neighbourhood of what appeared to be an old summer-house, now neglected and disused, for it was thickly overgrown with ivy and various creepers. Looking up close to it they observed a board, on which was painted in large letters, "Whoever is found trespassing in these grounds will be punished with the utmost rigour of the law." Scarcely had they read this unpleasant announcement, when they observed at the farther end of the walk a party of men, who from their costume were evidently huntsmen or game-keepers, led by a person whom they recognised at a glance as Mynheer Bunckum, their jealous rival.

"There are the robbers! There are the impostors! There are those thieves and vagabonds, who have come here pretending to be noblemen travelling for their pleasure. On! on! seize them, my men! treat them with no ceremony."

Mynheer Bunckum, though he shouted, did not move himself, and his followers appeared to hesitate for a few moments. This gave time to the Count and Baron to retreat behind the summer-house.

"Come along, Count, we must trust to our legs to escape from these fellows," cried the Baron, and he set off running as fast as he could go.

"Stop! stop!" cried the Count. "You will be seen to a certainty and overtaken; come in here, I perceive an opening, and we shall be able to lie hid, while our jealous rival passes by."

·The Baron, however, did not hear him, but still rushed on.

"I shall be seen if I attempt to run," thought the Count. Without more ado he slipped through an opening in the side of the wall, in his hurry forgetting to feel his way. He had made but a few steps when, to his dismay, he found himself descending, and fully believed that he was about to be precipitated down a well. Greatly to his relief he reached the bottom sooner than he had expected.

"Here, at all events, I shall be secure while our jealous rival and his men are hunting about for me; but I am afraid the Baron has very little chance of escaping. I might have got into rather a pleasanter place; it is somewhat damp; I hear the frogs croaking, and feel the slippery efts and other creatures crawling about. I only hope that there are no venomous snakes; but, by the by, how am I ever to get out again? We should have acted more wisely had we walked up boldly to Mynheer Bunckum, and apologising for having entered his grounds, wished him good morning. It is entirely owing to the Baron's cowardice that I am placed in this very unpleasant position."

Such were the thoughts which passed through the Count's mind, for he did not speak them aloud. He heard the voices of Mynheer Bunckum and his men, as they searched round and round the building, but none of them looked into the well, or if they

did, failed to discover him. At length, to his great
relief, their voices grew less and less distinct, and
he was satisfied that they were moving on.

"At all events this delay will have enabled the
Baron to make his escape, and I hope that by
and by, when these people have given up the search,
I shall be able to rejoin him," he thought.

Meantime the Baron had continued his course.
Not being much accustomed to running, he soon
began to puff and blow, and wish that he could
find some place in which to hide himself, and
recover his wind. Instead of taking the direct path
along which he and the Count had come, rightly
suspecting that if he did so he should quickly be
observed, he turned aside to a wilder part of the
wood ; he stopped every now and then to try and
recover his breath, and to ascertain if the Count
was following. Having no landmark to direct him,
he completely lost himself, and became very uncertain whether he was making his way out of the
wood, or only getting further into it.

"It was very selfish and unmannerly in Count

Funnibos not to accompany me," he said to him-self. "We might have helped each other out of this difficulty; and, indeed, at any moment Mynheer Bunckum and his myrmidons may overtake me, and in the vicious mood they are in, I do not know how I shall be treated. Ah! there I see a large hollow tree. Yes, there is an opening at the bottom, I will creep in and try to conceal myself within the stem till the hue and cry is over."

Suiting the action to the word, the Baron knelt down, and was about to crawl into the opening when he saw a movement of the bushes at a little distance off, and presently a head popped up above them.

"I hope that I was not observed," he thought, and he quickly crawled in at the hole, unfortunately, as he did so, knocking off his hat, which rolled away on one side; he dared not crawl out again to look for it, and could only hope that it would be con-cealed by the tall grass and underwood which grew around. The Baron stood trembling and quaking in his boots, every moment expecting to be discovered,

while he felt sure that the face of which he had caught a glimpse was no other than that of the jealous rival.

He listened anxiously; he could hear the crack-ing of the boughs, and then the sound of footsteps approaching. Nearer and nearer drew the footsteps; presently he heard an exclamation of surprise.

"Why, this is the hat of one of them," said a voice.

"Yes; it is that of the fat, ridiculous little man who pretended to be a Baron," answered a female voice.

Was it possible? Yes, the Baron felt sure that the voice was that of the fair Vrouw Margaret on whom he had placed his affections.

"Little doubt whose hat it is," observed the first speaker. "Very likely his pockets are even now full of your father's and Mynheer Baskerville's plate. What shall we do with him if we catch him?"

"I must leave him to your tender mercies," said Vrouw Margaret. "As he deceived us so grossly I cannot plead for him. Punish him as you think fit, and then let him go, if he will promise not to come near our house again."

"We have not caught him yet, though," observed Mynheer Bunckum. "But here come my men, and we'll make a thorough search in the neighbour-hood."

The Baron at this trembled more and more; while Mynheer Bunckum and Vrouw Margaret were speaking he heard several other persons approaching, who had, he judged by the remarks they let fall, been searching in vain for the Count. No one seemed to remark the hole in the tree; indeed, probably judging by the Baron's figure, they did not suppose that he could have crawled into it.

"The chances are the two went off together," remarked one of the keepers, "and by this time they are well out of the park."

"But what about this head-piece?" said Mynheer Bunckum, holding up the Baron's hat.

"He may have dropped it in his flight," said the keeper.

"If that is the case, we ought to be still pursuing them," said Mynheer Bunckum. "On, my men, and bring them back to me dead or alive! Come, Vrouw Margaret, we will continue our ramble; really, it is scarcely worth while to

take so much trouble about the capture of these
contemptible people, were it not to recover your
father's and Mynheer Baskerville's plate."

They had gone but a short distance when they
observed one of the keepers returning.

" I must hurry on the others," said Mynheer
Bunckum. " Stay but a moment, my fair Vrouw,
and I will return to you," he said, and hastened
away.

Just then a shout fell on the ear of Vrouw
Margaret, and she made her way in the direction
from which it proceeded, when looking over the
bushes she caught sight of the keeper dragging on
the unfortunate Baron by the collar of his coat.
The keeper was a knowing fellow, a strong, sturdy
Frieslander. Suddenly it struck him that the Baron,
in spite of his rotund figure, might have crept into
the hole at the bottom of the old oak; and as the
Baron's hat had been found near it, he divined,
and truly, that it had been knocked off while the
Baron was creeping in. He accordingly had gone
back for the purpose of ascertaining whether his

suspicions were correct.   Putting in his hand, he
felt one leg, then he felt another.   The Baron in
vain tried to draw them up out of the way; the
sturdy Frieslander hauled and hauled much in the
same way as he would have pulled a snake out of
its hole, and dragged the hapless Baron out of the
hollow tree.

"I have got you, Mynheer, have I?" he said,
looking at the Baron's pale countenance.   "Why
did you hide? Honest men do not try to conceal
themselves.   Come along, and answer for yourself
to Mynheer Bunckum, and tell us what has become
of your companion."

The Baron was too much alarmed to reply or to
offer any resistance; indeed, in the grasp of the
sturdy Frieslander it would have been useless, so
like a lamb he accompanied his captor.   Suddenly,
however, he saw a fair face looking over the bushes
—it was that of the Vrouw Margaret.   The sight
aroused all the manhood within him; he knew
himself to be innocent, he knew that the treatment
he was receiving was owing to the ill-feeling of a

jealous rival. He determined to show that he
would not submit tamely to be ill-treated, and
suddenly starting forward he endeavoured to free
himself from the grasp of his captor. A fatal
resolution—the Frieslander in a moment tripped up
his heels, and down he fell with his face on the
ground, while the Frieslander knelt over him
exclaiming—

"You will escape me, will you! you are mistaken,
Mynheer;" and, his anger aroused, seizing the
Baron by the hair, he rubbed his face in the
muddy ground.

In vain the Baron tried to free himself, in vain
he tried to cry out; the moment he opened his
mouth, down went his face again into the mud
till he was well-nigh suffocated.

"Will not you, Vrouw Margaret, have pity on
me? Will you not interfere to save me from this
cruel indignity?" he exclaimed, but the Vrouw
Margaret calmly watched the proceedings of the
sturdy Frieslander as if she highly approved of
them.

"Will you go along quietly?" asked the Frieslander, after he had subjected the Baron for some
minutes to this disagreeable treatment. "Say 'yes,'
or 'no;' for, if you say
'no,' be prepared for an-
other mouthful of mud."

"Yes, yes; I will go!"
cried the Baron, the con-
duct of the fair Vrouw
cutting him to the heart.

"Well, then, I will let

you get up; but remember, the instant you attempt to release yourself, down you go again, and perhaps in a less pleasant place than the last." Saying this the sturdy Frieslander placed the Baron on his legs.

"Come, you must wash the mud off your face in yonder pool," said the Frieslander, "for you look more ridiculous than you can well imagine."

The Baron accepted his captor's offer, for not only his mouth and nostrils, but his very eyes were filled with mud.

"Come, you look a little less ridiculous now," said the Frieslander with a taunting laugh, as he led the Baron past the spot where Vrouw Margaret was standing. In vain the Baron stretched out his hands and entreated her to plead for him, but she turned aside her head, and his captor dragged him along till they met Mynheer Bunckum and the rest of his men.

"I have got one of them!" cried the Frieslander. "What is to be done with him? I have not yet examined his pockets, so cannot say whether the stolen plate is in them."

"We will soon ascertain that," said Mynheer Bunckum.

The unfortunate Baron Stilkin was subjected to the indignity of being searched. Only such ordinary things as a gentleman carries about with him were discovered in the Baron's pockets, but certainly no silver forks or spoons.

"And where is your companion? asked Mynheer Bunckum in an authoritative tone.

"I know no more than the man in the moon. I parted from him when we read the notice that trespassers on this estate would be prosecuted; till then we did not know that we were trespassing, but on discovering that such was the case, we were retiring when, your shouts alarming us, we proceeded farther than we should otherwise have done."

"Then you say you know nothing about the so-called Count Funnibos?"

"I know nothing about the real Count Funnibos, for real he is, as I am a real Baron!" cried the ill-treated noble, his spirits rising once more. "I conclude that he is by this time out of these grounds, and on his way to the inn where we are residing; and I must beg you to understand, Mynheer, that we shall forthwith proceed to the Hague, and lay a formal complaint before our Ambassador of the way in which we distinguished foreigners have been treated."

"I will take the consequences," answered Mynheer Bunckum; and turning to his servants, he said, "We have no evidence against the man; conduct him to the confines of the estate, and with such kicks as you feel disposed to bestow, let him go his way."

"I protest, I loudly protest against this treatment!" cried the Baron.

But the sturdy Frieslander with his companions, utterly regardless of all the Baron could say, dragged him along till they reached the outskirts of the estate, when, placing him before them, they bade him run for his life, which to the best of his power he endeavoured to do to save himself from the kicks they had threatened to bestow. On he ran, not once looking behind him, followed by the derisive laughter of the sturdy Frieslander and his companions.

CHAPTER XIV.

MYNHEER BUNCKUM'S head butler or steward, a person who was looked upon with great respect on account of the embroidered coat he wore, was passing, shortly after the events narrated in our last chapter, the ruined building in which the Count, unable to release himself, still lay concealed, when a groan reached his ear. Not being a believer in ghosts or goblins, on hearing it he exclaimed, " Oh, oh! that's a human voice; somebody must have tumbled down the well. Whoever that somebody is, I will get him out; but how that is to be done is the question." He hunted about till he discovered a hay-rake with a long handle. " This will serve me as a fishing rod, and I should not

be surprised to find a fish at the end of it." The steward accordingly went to an opening in the wall just above the well; he plunged down the rake and quickly brought it up without anything at the end. "I must try again," he said, and he passed it round the wall. "I have got something now," he exclaimed, and he began to haul away. "A heavy fish at all events," he cried out. Though a muscular man, as most Frieslanders are, he had a hard job to haul up the rake. At last, stooping down, his hand came in contact with the collar of a man's coat. He hauled and hauled away; his rake had caught in the hyacinthine locks of Count Funnibos, whose countenance of a cadaverous hue now came in sight.

"Ho, ho!" cried the steward. "Who are you, may I ask?"

The Count was too much exhausted and alarmed to make any answer, and even when the steward set him on his legs, he had to lean against the ivied wall to support himself.

"You are the person, I have a notion, who has been giving us all this trouble," said the steward, looking the Count in the face. "If so, come along with me, and my master, Mynheer Bunckum, will know what to say to you."

Q

"I had no intention of giving you or any one else any trouble," answered the Count, when he at last found words to express himself. "I am much obliged to you for pulling me out of that dreadful hole, and shall be still further obliged if you will brush my clothes, and then conduct me through these grounds so that I may return to my hotel, which I am anxious to reach this evening."

The steward on hearing this, instead of acceding to the Count's request, burst into a loud fit of laughter.

"Ho, ho, ho! Very likely indeed," he answered. "You must come along with me into the presence of Mynheer Bunckum, and he will settle how to dispose of you."

"But I have no wish to see Mynheer Bunckum," said the Count; "indeed, I have a decided objection to do so. He has allowed the most unjust suspicions to take possession of his mind."

"I care not a pin for your objections," said the steward. "Come along with me, I can waste no further time: come along, I say;" and the steward laying hold of the Count by one arm, and the collar of his coat with the other hand, walked him along the path towards the castle in the fashion policemen are wont to treat offenders in the streets of London. The Count was too weak from hunger, alarm, and fatigue to offer any resistance, and allowed himself to be conducted in the direction the steward chose to go. They soon reached the castle; the steward, on inquiring for Mynheer Bunckum, was informed that he had gone out with the fair daughters of Mynheer Van Arent.

"Then there is but one thing to be done," observed the steward. "We must lock up this stranger in the dungeon till our master returns. Where are the keys?" They were quickly brought to him, and aided by the domestics of the establishment, he led the Count down a flight of stone steps to the dungeon.

"My friend," said the Count, who was beginning to recover, "this is very extraordinary treatment, but I presume you are acting under orders. I have a request to make. I am very hungry, and shall feel grateful if you will bring me some food; and, as I scarcely know otherwise how to pass the period of my incarceration, I shall be still further obliged if you will supply me with a violin, should you have such an instrument in the castle."

"Ho, ho, ho!" laughed the steward. "Then you are a strolling musician, as we have heard it reported. Well, we happen to have a violin, for I play it myself, and you shall be supplied with food, as I conclude Mynheer Bunckum would not wish to starve you to death."

"Thank you, my good friend, I am much obliged to you for your promise; at the same time, I beg leave to remark that I am not a strolling musician, but am as I represent myself, Count Funnibos."

"That is neither here nor there," said the steward, "you shall have the food and you shall have the violin; now please go down those steps, and make yourself as much at home as you like."

Finding resistance useless, the Count descended the steps into a large vaulted chamber, which appeared from the contents on which the light fell through the open door, to be used as a lumber-room or store-room rather than as a prison.

"Is this a fit place in which to thrust a gentleman?" said the Count, feeling his dignity considerably hurt. "Had it been a dungeon, with chains and bolts and bars, it would have been only such as many an unfortunate nobleman has been compelled to inhabit. But to be treated as if I were a piece of lumber is unbearable."

"We have no such refined opinions in this country, Mynheer," said the steward, with a grin on his countenance. "But make yourself happy, there is a chest for you to sit on and another on which your supper shall be placed. As to your bed and bedding we will see about that by-and-by, and the violin you ask for shall be brought forthwith. Perhaps in return you will favour me with a tune, as I am a lover of music, and shall be pleased to hear you play."

The Count, who, though not very wise in all matters, made the best of everything, sat himself down on the chest with folded arms to consider how, under the disagreeable circumstances in which

he was placed, it would be best to act. "One thing
is very clear, that Mynheer Bunckum has got the
upper hand of me. The best thing I can do as
soon as I obtain my liberty is to take my departure.
The fair Isabelle may or may not care a stiver for
me, and if she does not I must wish her farewell
and try to forget her charms."

Just as he had arrived at this wise resolution the
door opened, and the steward reappeared with a violin
in his hand, followed by a servant bringing a very
respectable supper.

"Thank you, my friend, thank you," said the
Count, getting up; "I should be happy to show you
my gratitude at once by playing a tune, but I think
that I shall play with more spirit after I have par-
taken of this food, for, as you may suppose, I am
pretty well starved."

"I shall be happy to await your pleasure," said
the steward, who was struck by the Count's polite
manner, and lifting up the dish-covers he helped
him liberally to the contents of the dishes. The
Count, considering all things, did ample justice to

the meal set before him, as well as to a bottle of Rhenish wine.

"I might have been worse off," he observed, greatly revived. "And now you shall have a tune."

Whereon, taking the fiddle and screwing up the keys, he began to play in a way which astonished the Friesian steward.

"Really, you are a master of the art, Mynheer," he observed. "Such notes have never before proceeded from that violin."

"I am happy to please you," answered the Count. "And now I must beg you, as soon as your master returns, to request that he will either set me at liberty and have me conveyed safely back to my hotel, or else give me better accommodation than this vault offers for the night."

The steward faithfully promised to carry out the Count's wishes, and, observing that he had duties to attend to, took his leave. The Count then, resuming his violin, once more began to play; the tunes he chose were such as especially suited his present feelings; they were of a gentle, pathetic character, often mournful and touching. He played on and on. Little was he aware who was listening to them. Could he have looked through the thick walls of his dungeon, he would have beheld a female form, her handkerchief to her eyes, leaning on the parapet of a terrace which ran along one of its sides. The lady whose tender feelings he had excited was no other than Isabelle Van Arent, who, with her sister and father and mother, had come that afternoon to pay a visit to Mynheer Bunckum. At length the Count ceased playing, and the lady tore herself away from the spot to rejoin her family, to whom she could not refrain from speaking of the pathetic music to which she had been listening.

"Oh, that must have been my steward, Hans Gingel. I know he plays the fiddle," observed Mynheer Bunckum, "and he sometimes goes to some out-of-the-way corner that he may not disturb the rest of the household, who are not generally inclined to be enraptured by his music."

"But he must, I assure you, be a very good player," urged the fair Isabelle.

"I dare say he can manage to produce a few good notes sometimes," said Mynheer Bunckum, in a careless tone. "Probably distance lent enchantment to the sound. I will not advise you to allow him to play very near at hand."

Vrouw Isabelle looked puzzled, and began to fancy that her ears had deceived her; at all events,

the Count had not obtained the advocate he might
have gained, had she known who was the hidden
musician to whom she had been listening. Mynheer
Bunckum waited till his guests were gone, when he
summoned his steward, Hans Gingel. "Has anything been heard of the other stranger?" he asked.

"I have him safe enough in the dungeon,"
answered the steward. "He is not a bad fellow
after all, as he takes the way he has been treated
with wonderful good humour." And the steward
described the mode in which he had hauled the
Count out of the well. "He is a rare player, too,
on the violin, and I lent him mine to amuse
himself with."

"Then it was not your music with which Vrouw
Isabelle was so delighted just now," observed
Mynheer Bunckum.

"No, no, no!" answered the steward laughing,
"my strains are not calculated to draw tears from
a lady's eyes; to tell you the truth, Mynheer, I
believe he is a Count after all."

"His playing only agrees with the story of his

being a travelling musician," observed Mynheer
Bunckum.

"But travelling musicians are not as polite and
well-mannered as our prisoner," said the steward.
"I know a gentleman when I meet him."

"But supposing he is a real Count, and the
other fellow who was so unceremoniously kicked
out of the place is a Baron, I may be somewhat in
a scrape," said Mynheer Bunckum.

"I will enable you to get out of it, then," said
Hans Gingel. "Let me visit the prisoner, and propose to him to make his escape. He has really won
my regard, and I should be glad, were it not dis-
pleasing to you, to set him at liberty. He will only
be too happy, I suspect, to get away, and will
probably not trouble you, or the family of Mynheer
Van Arent, any longer by his presence."

"But I accused him and his companion of
stealing the plate at the picnic, and I certainly do
not know who else could have taken it," said
Mynheer Bunckum.

"As to that, I am sure he is incapable of such

an act, and he would not associate with any person who was. I am, therefore, of opinion that neither he nor the Baron stole the plate; indeed, one of the men on board the yacht told me that he observed a boat with several boys approach the shore during the picnic, and that they climbed up the bank, as he supposed, to amuse themselves by watching what was going forward, or to obtain a few cakes or sweetmeats which any of the party might be disposed to give them. Now, since the plate is missing, it is much more than probable that those young monkeys took it, and, if search is made in the village, probably it will be found that they were the thieves."

"That alters the whole complexion of affairs," observed Mynheer Bunckum. "I am satisfied that the Baron, if such he is, will not become my rival, and Vrouw Isabelle is free to choose whom she will; therefore by all means set the Count at liberty as you propose, only don't let him know that I am aware of what you are doing, and advise him and his companion to take their departure from this part of the country as soon as possible."

" I will carry out your orders, Mynheer," was the answer. The steward waited, however, till night closed in, when, with a lantern in hand, he repaired to the dungeon.

"Count Funnibos," he said, "for such I believe you truly are, your music, and your manners, and your gentle behaviour have completely won my heart; and as I took you prisoner under what, you will allow, were somewhat suspicious circumstances, I must give myself the privilege of setting you free; and if you will consent to leave as I advise, you may do so without difficulty or danger, and by to-morrow morning be far beyond the reach of those whom you may look upon as enemies."

The Count thought for some moments before he replied. He recollected that he had been unjustly imprisoned, accused of robbery, and insulted by the lord of the mansion; but it would save a vast deal of trouble to himself and everybody else if he were to go away and let the matter drop. He quickly, therefore, decided on the latter course.

"I accept your offer, my friend," he answered. "When shall we set out?"

"I would advise you, Count, to wait for some hours, till everyone is in bed, and there is no risk of your being discovered and followed. I will then come for you, and conduct you down to the river, where you will find numerous boats in which you can cross the Meer, and soon make your way to the seaboard; and thence either proceed to Amsterdam by water, or go across the Zuyder Zee to Hoorn, or any other place on its shore."

"Your plan just suits my fancy," said the Count. "But my friend and companion, Baron Stilkin, what will become of him?"

"You can write and tell him to join you at whatever place you may happen to reach," said Hans Gingel. "It would cause considerable delay were you to go back to your inn."

The Count thought the matter over, and reflected

that it would be very pleasant to enjoy a few days of independent action.

"I have an idea," he said to the steward. "I will write a note to Baron Stilkin desiring him to return to Amsterdam, and to wait for me there, if you will undertake to have it delivered."

"Very gladly, Mynheer," answered Hans Gingel. "I will get you paper and pens. Now, if you can rest in tolerable comfort propped up between these chests, I will come for you at the hour named, and as you may grow hungry, bring you some more food to stay your appetite." The note to the Baron was written, the Count discussed the second supper, and, having recovered from his fatigue, was perfectly ready, when the steward appeared, to make his escape from the castle.

"Tread softly," said the steward, as he led the way up the steps. "It is important not to awaken Mynheer Bunckum or any of the servants. I have shut up the dogs, so that they will not bark unless they hear a noise."

Cautiously they proceeded, the steward holding a

lantern and the Count following close at his heels. They were soon out of the dungeon, when the steward, turning to the right, led the way along a narrow passage which conducted them to the opposite side of the building. The steward then, producing a key from his pocket, opened a door, the lock gliding back smoothly as if it had been well oiled, they passed on, and the Count found himself in the open air.

"We are now outside the castle," whispered the steward; "but should Mynheer Bunckum look out of his window he might perhaps fancy that we are thieves, and fire off his blunderbuss at our heads; so be cautious, and do not speak above a whisper till we get to a distance."

"I am afraid that I shall not be able to find my way in the dark," whispered the Count.

"Do not be anxious on that subject," answered the steward. "I intend to accompany you till day breaks, and see you safe on the high road." They walked on and on till day began to dawn. The fresh morning air revived the Count's spirits, and he was more than ever satisfied with himself at the thoughts of starting on an independent tour without the company of the Baron.

"I will buy a gun, and a knapsack, and a telescope, and a shooting-dress, and will trudge across the country, living on the produce of the chase. I saw a vast number of birds as we came along on the canals and borders of the Meers, and I shall have no lack of sport. Such a life suits my present mood."

"A very excellent plan," observed the steward; "but I would advise you to employ some more rapid means of locomotion than your own legs afford till you get to a distance from this. Mynheer Bunckum may be wandering about in the neighbourhood, and should he fall in with you the consequences may be disagreeable."

"I will take your advice, my friend," said the Count; "but I must first procure the gun and the telescope, the knapsack and the shooting-dress."

"Certainly, and I shall be happy to assist you in that object. We can at once proceed to Sneek,

R

which being one of the chief places of the province of Friesland, everything you require can be procured."

"I am overwhelmed by your kindness, and I accept your offer," said the Count. And they proceeded on their way, having stopped to breakfast at a house of a friend of the steward.

They reached Sneek about noon. The articles the Count required were speedily procured.

"And now farewell, my friend," he said, taking the steward's hand. "We are brothers of the bow, and I look upon you as a friend who has rendered me an essential service, although you did haul me out of the well in a somewhat rough fashion."

The steward made an appropriate answer, and they parted—he to return to Bunckum Castle, the Count to proceed to the southward.

CHAPTER XV.

THE Count, as evening approached, reached the borders of a Meer a short distance from the Zuyder Zee. It was fringed by trees and by tall reeds almost as high as the trees, which grew partly in the water and partly out of it.

"If I could find a boat I might take a passage in her to the other side of the Meer, and thus continuing my journey obtain rest at the same time," he thought.

He hunted about, and at last found a path, at the further end of which he observed a barge with her bows run into the bank. Having left his knapsack and gun on the bank, he stepped on board, thinking that some of the crew might appear. Seeing no one, he was again going on shore, when the after hatch was flung open and three

huge heads adorned by night-
caps, with big staring eyes
expressive of wonder, popped up, each face being
more ugly than the other.

"Who are you?" asked the first.

"What business have you on board here?" inquired a second.

"Where do you come from, where do you want to go?" asked a third, the ugliest of all three.

"Really, gentlemen," said the Count, bowing, for he was always polite, "you overwhelm me with questions. My object is to cross the Meer, or to get to some inn or farmhouse where I may pass the night in comfort."

"Ho, ho, ho!" exclaimed the last speaker. "You will not find any inn or farmhouse where you can pass the night on the borders of this Meer, but we'll give you a passage to the other end, for which we are bound when we have had our suppers, always provided you are willing to pay for it."

"Certainly," replied the Count. "I am willing to pay for everything I obtain. Your barge looks like a very safe one, and I will therefore engage a passage."

"Safe! I should think she was safe," answered

the ugly individual. "It would require a gale to upset her with all sail hoisted. Trust Captain Jan Dunck for that."

Upon this the Count looked harder than before at the ugly man's countenance. "What, are you Captain Jan Dunck?" he inquired.

"No doubt about that, though I do not command so large a craft as formerly," said the ugly man. "If I mistake not, you are Count Funnibos, whom I, once upon a time, brought round from Antwerp, and landed at Amsterdam."

"No, you did not land me at Amsterdam," answered the Count; "you landed me on the island of Marken, when you played that scurvy trick upon poor Pieter. I thought that you had been lost."

"So I nearly was, for the *Golden Hog* went down, but my mate and small ship's boy were saved. Here is one of them."

The mate gave a wink of recognition.

"So you want me to carry you across the lake —is that it?" continued the skipper.

"Such is my wish," said the Count, though, at

the same time, he felt very doubtful about trusting himself and his fortunes to Captain Jan Dunck.

"Well, we'll get under weigh immediately," said the skipper. "Though there is no wind, we can pole the barge a considerable part of the distance."

"But I must first get my luggage, my fowling-piece, my knapsack, and telescope," said the Count.

"Well, be sharp about it," answered the skipper. "Time and tide wait for no man."

"But there is no tide in this lake, and you did not appear to be in a hurry when I came on board," said the Count.

"For the best of reasons, we were fast asleep," answered the skipper, as the Count went for his luggage, which neither the skipper, the mate, nor the crew offered to carry for him. He therefore brought it on board himself, for he had become wonderfully independent during his travels. He sat himself down on his knapsack, expecting that the skipper would at once get under weigh; but that individual, instead of doing so, dived again below, followed by his mate and his crew, to discuss some supper which they had stowed away in a locker.

While the Count sat awaiting the return of the skipper and his crew on deck, he observed another boat in the distance, in which was a single man. The person appeared to have been watching the barge, and now cautiously approached, using a paddle, so as to make as little noise as possible. He was apparently about to address the Count when the skipper popped up his head, with his mouth full of food, on which the stranger immediately began to row away in an opposite direction.

"Hilloa, you! have you anything to say to me? If not, keep your distance, or you will have to smart for it!" shouted the skipper.

The stranger made no reply, but rowed slowly away, and Captain Jan Dunck again dived into the cabin. The stranger then stopped, and made a sign to the Count. Soon afterwards the mate and the crew, returning on deck, cast off the rope which secured the barge to the bank, and taking up some long spars, began to pole out into the lake, while the skipper sat at the helm smoking his pipe. He smoked and smoked as he used to do on board the *Golden Hog*, but did not invite the Count to join him. After some time the water became too deep for poling, and the mate and the crew took to their oars. The water was calm, and there appeared to be no possibility of danger; but yet the Count did not feel altogether comfortable.

"And so you say that one-eyed Pieter threatened to bring me to justice?" growled Captain Jan Dunck.

"I said nothing of the sort," answered the Count; "I told you that the Baron and I took one-eyed Pieter on board our boat. Had he been drowned, you would have been guilty of his death; and you ought to be thankful to me for saving you from committing so great a crime."

"Ho, ho, ho!" laughed the skipper, and his mate and crew laughed in chorus. After the crew had rowed for some time, an island appeared in view, with dunes, or sandhills, rising over a considerable portion. It was a barren-looking spot, as far as the Count could judge in the fast increasing gloom of night.

"We are going to put into the shore there," said the skipper, pointing to it. "If you take my advice, you will land."

"But that is not the sort of place to which I wish to go," said the Count. "My object on board your barge was to take a passage to some habitable region, where I could obtain food, rest, and shelter."

"The sea-gulls will afford you plenty of food; as to rest, you can lie down on the sand; and as for shelter, your pocket-handkerchief will afford you as much as you are likely to find."

"I protest against being so treated," said the Count, naturally growing indignant.

"To whom do you protest," asked the skipper, "to me or my crew? There's no one else to hear you, and we do not care the snuff of a candle for your protestations."

The mate and the crew uttered not a word.

"I must submit to my hard destiny," thought the Count; "I have not made a very brilliant commencement of my sporting adventures, but I set out with the intention of shooting birds, and apparently the island abounds with them."

In a short time the barge touched the sandy beach.

"You will step on shore, Count Funnibos," said the skipper, with an ill-favoured grin on his countenance.

"But I have paid my passage-money, and I protest."

"We settled that point some time ago," said the skipper; "you will step on shore, as I have just remarked."

The Count looked at the mate and the crew. Their countenances wore the same ill-favoured expression as did that of the skipper. They merely placed a plank from the bow of the barge to the beach.

"You will walk along the plank, Count Funnibos," said the skipper.

The Count took up his knapsack, his gun, and his telescope, and, shrugging his shoulders with as dignified an air as he could assume, obeyed. The moment he had set foot on the island, the plank was withdrawn and his retreat cut off. Directly afterwards the mate and the crew shoved the barge away from the shore, and began rowing as before, while the skipper resumed his seat at the helm, and puffed calmly from his pipe, as if he had just performed some meritorious act. A few sea-birds came flying in with loud cries and shrieks from their daily fishing excursions over the waters, but they would not have afforded him a palatable meal even if he had shot one of them.

"The sand is soft, that is one comfort," he thought; "and there are no wild beasts, wolves, or bears to trouble me; it might have rained, or there might have been a strong cold wind, or I might have been more hungry than I am; so I might have been worse off. A boat of some sort will probably be passing during the day and take me off. I may at present consider myself very like that great hero, Robinson Crusoe, or any other mariner who has been wrecked or marooned on a desert island."

These sort of thoughts occupied his mind till he fell fast asleep. Having had a long walk the previous day, he was more tired than usual, and did not once wake during the whole night. The rays of the rising sun glaring into his eyes aroused him, and he sprang to his feet, feeling rather stiff and somewhat chilled, for the night had been cold. He climbed to the top of a sand-hill, that he might take a wider survey. Scarcely had he reached it than he observed a boat approaching the shore. Putting down his gun and knapsack, he took out his telescope, and that he might steady it, stretched himself on the side of the sand-hill. Having adjusted the focus, he directed it towards the boat. She came nearer and nearer. He saw that she contained several people, who seemed to have the intention of landing.

"I shall now be able to escape from this," he thought.

As the boat approached he could clearly distinguish the features of those in her. He could not

be mistaken ; three were ladies — the Vrouw Van Arent and her two daughters; three were gentlemen — Mynheer Van Arent, Mynheer Bunckum, and a stranger. They helped the ladies out of the boat, and then all six walked along the beach. The stranger offered his arm to the fair Isabelle, which she took with evident willingness. Mynheer Bunckum walked on with Vrouw Margaret, and the old couple followed.

"No, I cannot join them. I cannot so demean myself as to ask for a passage to the shore," muttered the Count. "I only hope that they will not discover me. I shall certainly not discover myself, if I can help it."

If curiosity had brought the party to the island, they were soon satisfied, for in a short time they re-embarked, and the Count had lost his chance of escaping for that time.

"It is better that it should be so," he said. "I should only have had to answer disagreeable questions, and perhaps have subjected myself to .further indignities."

Hunger now compelled him to seek for food, and loading his gun, he looked out for a bird which might come within range, but the birds all kept at a wary distance. He observed, further to the south, that the island was very much lower, and that the birds frequented it in greater numbers; he

accordingly bent his
steps in that direction.
It appeared level, and,
as far as he could judge, easy to walk over.   On
reaching it, however, he found that it was sprinkled

with so many shallow pools that he would speedily wet his boots through, therefore, sitting down on the first dry spot he came to, he pulled them off and hung them over his shoulders.

"Come, I feel something like a sportsman now," he said to himself.

Immediately afterwards a duck came quacking by within range. He fired, and, to his infinite satisfaction, brought it to the ground. He rushed eagerly forward to secure his prize, and although it went fluttering on for some distance, he succeeded in catching it, and, wringing its neck, hung it behind him.

"I need no longer fear dying of starvation, even although I may have to spend a day or two on this desert spot," he said to himself.

To his delight he brought down, before long, another duck, and was now thinking of returning to the higher ground, when he saw a boat passing near the further end of the low part of the island. He rushed forward to make a signal, hoping to attract the attention of those on board, but by the

time he had got to the point to which he was
directing his steps, the boat was at such a distance
that his signals could not be seen. On and on he
went ; the sea-fowl came shrieking and quacking
round him, when, to his dismay, he observed that
dark clouds were gathering in the sky, threatening
a storm of no gentle nature.

" This sort of work is all very well in fine
weather, but I have no fancy to be exposed to
drenching rain and howling wind," he said to
himself. " I must get back, at all events, to the
higher ground."

He had got so far from it, that this was no
easy matter. Before he had walked for many
minutes, down came the rain like a sheet of water,
driven against him by the fierce wind.

He had now good reason to be seriously alarmed.
The water in the pools, before scarcely up to his
ankles, now reached almost to his knees. " Can the
dykes have been burst through ?" he thought. " If
so, my fate is sealed—not only mine, but that of
numbers of the inhabitants of the surrounding

district." From the rapid way in which the surface of the Meer rose he felt convinced that this must be the case. Still the love of life compelled him to try and save himself, and he did not despair; although, as far as he could see, no means of making his escape were likely to present themselves.

CHAPTER XVI.

S he was hurrying on along the shore, he saw what looked to him like a wheelbarrow, with a heap of gourds or inflated skins, or some other roundish objects, though he could scarcely at the distance distinguish what they were. He reached the spot. "Come, at all events, if the waters rise, as I fear they will, these things will enable me to construct a raft on which I may manage to float on the troubled waters," he said to himself.

Lashing them together, he took his seat on the top of this curiously constructed raft. Scarcely had he done so, when the waters came rushing over the island, and carried him and his raft far away as they swept onward in their course. On and on he went, his very natural fear being that he should be carried into the Zuyder Zee; he soon, however, came in sight of land raised above the waters, on which he could distinguish cottages and other buildings.

"Well, this is a new style of navigation, but I ought to be thankful that I have got something to keep me above water," he said to himself.

He of course, as he glided on, was looking about in all directions, and he now caught sight in the distance of what he hoped was a boat. Again and again he cast his eager gaze at the object. Yes, it was a boat, and a man was in her; he waved his hat and shouted. As he approached, the Count looked at him; yes, he was, there could be no doubt about it, the one-eyed mariner, old Pieter, who shouted—

"Hold on, Mynheer! hold on! and I will soon be up to you."

"What, don't you know me?" asked the Count, as Pieter got near.

"Bless me, of course I do; and glad I am to have come to take you on board, or you might have been carried away into the Zuyder Zee, or somewhere else, for aught I can tell. When I saw you on board Captain Jan Dunck's vessel, I tried to get near enough to warn you that you must beware of him, as I felt sure that he would play you some scurvy trick or other. He has been going on from bad to worse, all owing to the. oceans of schiedam he has poured down that ugly mouth of his."

This was said when the Count was comfortably seated in the stern of Pieter's boat. There was another person on board whom the Count recognised as the small ship's boy, who had long been Pieter's faithful companion. He nodded and smiled his recognition, and seemed highly delighted at again meeting with the Count.

"And now where shall we go?" asked Pieter.

"To the nearest shore where I can obtain food and shelter, and change my wet garments," answered the Count.

"Well, you do look dampish," observed Pieter.

"Damp! I have been wet to the skin for these

hours past, and almost starved to death in the bargain," said the Count.

"Then I will lose no time in taking you to Meppel, or any other place we can most easily reach." And bending his back to the oars, the one-eyed mariner pulled away.

"'One good turn deserves another,' as the old saying is," observed Pieter, for he wanted to say something to keep up the Count's spirits. "You saved my life and gave me this boat, and now I have the satisfaction of saving yours."

"You are an honest fellow, Pieter, and as I prize honest men, of whom I have not discovered as many as I desire in the world, I should be glad if you and the small ship's boy will accompany me, and I will endeavour to obtain some post which I consider suited to your merits. Old Pieter gladly accepted the Count's offer, and it did not make him pull the less vigorously. All night long they rowed on, till they arrived at a part of the country which the flood had not reached. Here Pieter took the Count to the house of a farmer to whom the honest boatman was well known, having been on various occasions employed by him. The good farmer treated the Count with the utmost hospitality and kindness. It was some days, however, before the Count had sufficiently recovered to be once more himself, and able to extend his walks beyond the precincts of the farm. He had gone one day to some distance, when he saw a large and picturesque house rising amid an extensive shrubbery; an open gate invited him to enter. As he walked along he caught the sound of voices, and presently found himself in the presence of a party of gentlemen, seated round a table with books and papers before them. Conspicuous on one side was a large easel supporting a handsome picture. "Ah! this is something out of the way," thought the Count, and advancing he made a bow and introduced himself.

"You are welcome, noble Count, to our revels," said one of the gentlemen, who appeared to be the president. ".But ours is a feast of reason and the flow of soul, and we are met here to discuss works of art, to hear read the practical effusions of our members, and to enjoy the society of men of intellect and erudition."

"A very praiseworthy and satisfactory mode of passing time, and I am fortunate in having fallen into such good company," remarked the Count.

The various members of the society individually welcomed him. A poet had just read some verses he had composed, which were received with thundering applause, one of the excellent rules of the society being that every one was to praise the works of the rest. The artist now exhibited his paintings; when the others had admired them to their fill, the Count looked at them through his spectacles, and if he did make a mistake, and suppose that a horse was a cow, or a sheep a pig, he wisely kept his opinion to himself, merely exclaiming: "Beautiful! how true to nature. What exquisite colouring; what elegant outlines! yet all are equalled by the composition." As no one asked him to point out the individual excellencies of which he spoke, he was looked upon as a first-rate judge of art.

"Now, gentlemen, as our friend Scrubzen has not been able to-day to complete his grand picture, I am deputed to invite you to inspect it to-morrow, when it will be in a more forward state. We shall, I hope, be favoured by your presence, Count Funnibos?"

"By all means," answered the Count, who was highly pleased with the society into which he had fallen; and he parted from them to return to the house of his hospitable entertainer. The next morning he set out to repair to the house of which the president had given him the address.

"Several of Scrubzen's admirers have already arrived," said the president, whom he met at the door; "and with them a distinguished foreigner."

As the Count and the president entered, they saw at the further end of the room a large picture on an easel representing a coast scene. On one side stood the artist explaining the details of his painting; a number of ladies and gentlemen were gazing at it with admiring glances; but one figure especially attracted the attention of the Count. It

was, there could be no doubt
about it, Baron Stilkin, whom
he thought had long since
reached Amsterdam, or had
returned to his family mansion. Yes, it was the
Baron, not decreased in rotund proportions since

they parted. "Grand, very grand!" he exclaimed in sonorous tones, approaching the picture. "It reminds me forcibly of the best of Claude's productions; exquisite colouring!"

"And what is your opinion, Count Funnibos?" asked the President.

"He has grown wonderfully fat," answered the Count, who was thinking of the Baron. "I fear that no carriage can be found strong enough to take him home."

"I beg your pardon, Count, I was speaking of the picture," remarked the President. The Baron, however, had heard the Count's voice; turning round, he opened his arms to give him a friendly embrace.

"What, my dear Count! Is it you, yourself?

"I think you ran away and left me to my mysterious fate," said the Count, with a slight degree of stiffness. "I conclude that you did not receive my letter requesting you to meet me at Amsterdam, and stating the reasons for my not rejoining you sooner; however, I am very glad to see you again."

"No, indeed, I received no letter," answered the Baron. "Had I done so, it would have saved me a world of anxiety."

"We must remember that we are in the presence of strangers," said the Count. "Our friend here desired to know my opinion of that magnificent picture. I may add that it surpasses my utmost expectations."

His opinion highly pleased the artist as well as the spectators, who were delighted to find their countryman's production so highly praised by two distinguished foreigners.

"And now, Count," said the Baron, as they walked away arm in arm, "I am compelled to return home. My son, the hope of my house, is about to marry a lady whose magnificent fortune will retrieve the fallen fortunes of our family. Will you accompany me?"

"By all manner of means," answered the Count. "I have met with sufficient adventures, or rather misadventures, to satisfy me for the rest of my life. I have seen a large portion of Holland, if not the whole of it, and I am satisfied that it is as well worth seeing as any country in the world."

"Your decision gives me infinite satisfaction," answered the Baron. "We will go back to-morrow, and I hope that you will be present at the wedding of my beloved son. I would rather he married the lady himself, though she is of an age which might have been considered suitable to me."

The Count and the Baron travelled back, accompanied by Pieter and the small ship's boy, at a far greater speed than that at which they had performed their outward journey. The Count was greatly relieved that his castle and estates had not run away during his absence, although Johanna Klack, at the very hour of his arrival, gave him notice that she must give up his service.

"To-morrow is the day fixed for my dear son's wedding," said the Baron, who had called on the Count. "You will, I trust, honour him and me by your presence, and that of your household."

"By all means," said the Count. "I will come myself, and bring one-eyed Pieter and the small ship's boy. It will be a novel and interesting spectacle to them."

The Count and his attendants arrived. The happy bridegroom appeared dressed in the height of fashion, the hour for the nuptial party to set out had struck.

" I must go in and bring forth the bride," he said; and he soon reappeared with a female, holding a large bouquet in her hand. She wore a wreath of roses and a white veil over her head; her neck was long, so was her nose; her figure was the reverse of stout, but that in a youthful female is to be admired.

"Is that a mop-stick with clothes hung on it?" whispered the small ship's boy, as he gazed at the future Baroness.

"My dear Baron," said the Count, after he had made a profound bow to the lady, "how did your son manage to make up his mind?"

"I made it up for him," answered the Baron "He is a dutiful son, and does whatever I tell him. Suppose we change the subject, and when the nuptials are over, what do you say to setting out again on our travels? I shall be as ready as before to keep the accounts, and I hope to put a fair share into the common fund."

"I will think about it," said the Count. "At present, I have had travelling enough to satisfy me for some time to come; and as Johanna Klack has left my service, I do not know into whose hands I can satisfactorily leave the charge of my castle and estates during my absence."

THE END.

UNWIN BROTHERS, PRINTERS, LONDON AND CHILWORTH.

www.ingramcontent.com/pod-product-compliance
Lightning Source LLC
Chambersburg PA
CBHW060604030726
47498CB00005B/1540